Totally Bound Publishing books by Bailey Bradford:

Southwestern Shifters

Rescued
Relentless
Reckless
Rendered
Resilience
Reverence
Revolution
Revenge

I0542410

Southern Spirits

A Subtle Breeze
When the Dead Speak
All of the Voices
Wait Until Dawn
Aftermath
What Remains
Ascension
Whirlwind
Reluctance

Love in Xxchange

Rory's Last Chance
Miles to Go
Bend
What Matters Most
Ex's and O's
A Bit of Me
A Bit of You
In My Arms Tonight
Where There's a Will

Leopard's Spots

Levi
Oscar
Timothy
Isaiah
Gilbert
Esau
Sullivan

Wesley
Nischal
Justice
Sabin
Cliff

Mossy Glenn Ranch
Chaps and Hope
Ropes and Dreams
Saddles and Memories
Fences and Freedom
Riding and Regrets
Broncs and Bullies

Yes, Forever
Yes, Forever: Part One
Yes, Forever: Part Two
Yes, Forever: Part Three
Yes, Forever: Part Four
Yes, Forever: Part Five

Spotless
Hide
Hunt
Home

Coyote's Call
Off Course

What's his Passion?
Unexpected Places
Unexpected Moments

Breaking the Devil
Dark Nights and Headlights
Texas and Tarantulas

What's his Passion?

UNEXPECTED MOMENTS

BAILEY BRADFORD

Unexpected Moments
ISBN # 978-1-78430-347-1
©Copyright Bailey Bradford 2014
Cover Art by Posh Gosh ©Copyright November 2014
Interior text design by Claire Siemaszkiewicz
Totally Bound Publishing

Published in 2014 by Totally Bound Publishing, Newland House, The Point, Weaver Road, Lincoln, LN6 3QN, United Kingdom.

Totally Bound Publishing is a subsidiary of Totally Entwined Group Limited.

UNEXPECTED
MOMENTS

Dedication

To my family and friends, I love you.
To everyone I work with at Totally Bound, thank you.
Y'all rock.

Chapter One

Carter tugged at his shirt cuffs. He shouldn't have been as nervous as he was, but his heart fluttered and his pulse raced. He touched his tie. Reassured it was straight and that he was as attractive as possible, he entered the restaurant.

The host glanced up at him and smiled warmly. "Good evening, sir. Are you meeting someone or dining alone?"

Carter's cheeks warmed. "Er, meeting someone. Carter Hausemann is the name the reservation is under. Another gentleman, Mr. Canales, will be joining me shortly." *I hope.*

The host nodded. He ran his finger down a paper in front of him then checked Carter's name off it. "There you are, right here. Very good, sir. I'm Rogelio and I'll be seating you tonight. Follow me, please."

There was no reason for him to be so edgy. He'd spoken with Eddie the night before and confirmed their plans. Still, Carter kept thinking, *what if.* They didn't really know each other, besides having had sex a few times.

Spectacular sex. And we did talk during the hiking trip. Carter had been stunned to discover the park ranger leading the group on the hiking adventure was one of the same men he'd hooked up with for a threesome just a couple of days earlier—the one man he'd really been into during that fun little orgy. Yes, Eddie Canales was everything Carter wanted in a man— hopefully. Carter had no problem imagining the two of them hiking along the Appalachian Trail. That was his dream vacation, the one thing he was determined to do above all else. He'd love to share the experience with Eddie.

"You could seat us both."

Carter turned and couldn't keep back a smile when he saw Eddie standing there. "Hey, you made it." He immediately felt like a fool for saying that. *My insecurity must be showing.* "You look good," he added, before Eddie could respond.

'Good' was an understatement. Eddie was sexy as hell in a black suit and blue shirt. No tie for him, which was fine. Carter liked the dressy-casual attire on Eddie almost as much as he liked him in leather or naked. Not quite, though.

"This way, sirs," Rogelio said. "I have the perfect table for you."

Carter gestured and waited for Eddie to step in front of him. Eddie gave a slight shake of his head. "No, after you." He leaned forward and whispered, "I want to watch you walk and see your cute ass move beneath that jacket. Think about what I'm gonna do to it, and you, later."

Carter sucked in a shaky breath as he flushed hot from his head to his feet. He couldn't meet Eddie's gaze or else his burgeoning erection might turn into a full-blown hard-on that even his suit jacket couldn't hide. Carter stepped back then turned to follow Rogelio.

Rogelio led them to a table set in the back corner. They were more secluded than if they'd been seated elsewhere, and Carter appreciated the privacy. "Thank you," he said, taking his seat.

Rogelio winked at him. "It isn't always easy in this town for men like us to have a romantic date."

There was no point in denying that he and Eddie were on a date. Rogelio wasn't likely to bash them, though Carter did understand the need for discretion in Odessa. As much as he'd like to be able to touch Eddie and kiss him if the mood struck, they couldn't be as free in public as straight couples could.

Eddie murmured a thank you to Rogelio.

"Mathias will be your waiter this evening. Can I start you off with one of our wines?" Rogelio handed them a thin drink menu, followed by the larger meal ones.

Carter and Eddie took them.

Carter deferred to Eddie. "Would you like to order, or…"

Eddie grinned. "I'd really like a beer, to tell the truth."

"Same," Carter agreed. "What do you have on tap?"

Rogelio took the wine listings back. "We have the usual line up — Bud, Bud Light, Miller and so on, or we have an excellent local brew, Dare's Pale Ale. It's been getting rave reviews. Dare's also has a stout that I would highly recommend."

"I'll try the stout," Eddie said.

Carter preferred a lighter beer. "The Pale Ale, please."

"Very good, sirs. Mathias will be right over with them." Rogelio left them.

"It's good to see you again," Eddie murmured, his gaze burning through Carter's nervousness. "It might seem too soon to say but the truth is, I've missed you."

That confession eradicated the rest of Carter's unease. "It's not too soon. I feel the same way."

Eddie shifted in his seat, leaning back and resting his folded hands on the table. "I wasn't sure. You seemed kind of uptight when I got here."

"I was afraid you'd change your mind." Carter rolled his eyes and groaned. "And now you know how insecure I am. Sorry. I swear I'm not usually so immature."

Eddie chuckled and surprised Carter by reaching across the table to hold his hand. "I worried you'd realize I'm just not good enough for you, so let's both admit we have faults and let it go. You're here, I'm here, and for what it's worth, I can tell you I never once thought of not showing up. You've been on my mind every day since I saw you two weeks ago."

"Oh." Carter was so pleased he figured he was beaming. "Same. I… This starting a new relationship thing is complicated."

"It'll be worth it." Eddie released his hand and sat back just as a waiter approached.

"Good evening, gentlemen. I'm Mathias and I'll be your waiter tonight." He set their beers on the table while he started naming off the specials, spending a solid minute extolling the virtues of the aged steaks that cost a ridiculous amount of money.

Carter's mouth watered. He was going to splurge since he'd been anticipating this date for two weeks. "Thank you. We'd like a few minutes to examine the menu."

After Mathias left them, Carter perused his options. "I think I'll have the aged steak. How about you? No pressure, of course. I just want to try it once in my life at least." And since they were going Dutch on the bill, he didn't feel bad about ordering it, either.

Eddie hummed and didn't answer right off the bat.

Carter liked the way he took his time and didn't seem to feel rushed. He thought Eddie was enjoying their date so far.

"I've had it before," Eddie finally said. "Not here, but at this place in Indiana. It was really good, too. So I'm hung up on ordering it or the surf and turf."

Carter gave an exaggerated glance around them, then whispered, "You have to wonder about the surf part of that since we're practically in the desert."

Eddie chuckled and closed the menu. "True enough, but I'm feeling daring tonight."

"Daring enough to risk the chance of botulism?" Carter asked, arching a brow at him.

Eddie arched one right back. "I doubt that'd be a possibility here."

"Probably not." Carter had only been teasing, and Eddie's expression let him know he was aware of it. "I've really been looking forward to seeing you again. It feels kind of weird being out like this after what we've done."

Eddie's smoldering expression had Carter's dick firming up fully. "What we've done has led us to understand we want something more. Although, I intend to be doing more of, well…you."

The cheesy line should have been laughable, but Eddie said it with so much sincerity that Carter considered forgoing their date to head back to his place instead.

"We know we're more than compatible in bed," Eddie continued, after a glance around. "That's a huge thing in a relationship and so far, what time we've spent talking shows that we do well there, too."

Carter didn't want to be a downer, but he knew how it always started in relationships. Everyone was on their best behavior, trying to win the other person over and once they did…people changed. He'd done it himself, back when he'd been younger. Of course, he and Eddie were both older, so maybe they were more comfortable in their own skin so far. Plus, they'd met at a club and immediately hooked up with a third man to have sex with. Perhaps they didn't have to pretend to be better than they were.

But Carter did wonder something. "How old are you?" He would have put Eddie in his mid-thirties. "Sorry if that's rude to ask."

Eddie waved the apology off. "It's not rude. Anything having to do with me is open for the inquisition." He winked. "I'm thirty-four. You?"

Carter's stomach went a little jittery from that wink. On all levels, Eddie just did it for him. "Thirty-one. Just had a birthday on the twelfth of last month."

"Oh really?" Eddie asked, amusement lighting up his features. "Well, I think you should get a belated birthday spa—" He cut himself off when Mathias suddenly appeared. "I'll have the surf and turf and another beer with it, along with a glass of water."

They'd been so tied up in each other that neither of them had noticed the waiter approaching. From the amusement clearly showing on Mathias' face, Carter thought the waiter might have heard enough of what Eddie had been saying to catch on about the spanking. Not that Mathias knew it was more than a joke, Carter reassured himself. Only Carter and Eddie knew he liked things rough.

"The aged steak, loaded baked potato and green beans, thank you." Carter handed over his menu. "I'll probably need another beer by then too and a small glass of water."

After Mathias left, Carter and Eddie resumed their conversation. It was a pleasant meal and the underlying sexual tension kept Carter's cock half-hard the whole time.

"What's your dream vacation?" Eddie asked him at one point.

Carter didn't have to think about it. "It'd take months to do it right, but I want to hike the Appalachian Trail." He chuckled and peeled part of the label off his beer bottle. "I'd have to be financially secure enough to take a leave of absence—or retire altogether—so I don't see it happening for a long time. That sucks, too, because I would prefer to hike it while I'm young and healthy, but with the economy and all, I might never get to do it."

Eddie nodded. "I know what you mean. I've always wanted to hike it, too, and Everest—that's on my bucket list."

"That's mountain climbing," Carter pointed out. "Quite different and more dangerous than hiking a trail."

"I think more people die while hiking than while mountain climbing," Eddie argued. "That could be because more people hike, sure, but we've had several die from heart attacks alone. Then there's falls, exposure, animals and snakes..." He shrugged. "I will admit that Everest is deadlier still, and it's a pipe dream anyway. I don't have much experience with real climbing, either. Not more than rock walls at the gym."

Carter tried not to shiver. "I know it's stupid, but the heights thing gets to me. Hiking is different. I don't really like trails that are on mountain ledges, though I can handle them. The idea of climbing up a mountain, that makes my skin crawl. You're a braver man than I am."

"Or a more foolish one," Eddie tucked his napkin under his plate. "Who knows? If I did actually try climbing a mountain, I might hate it. There are lots of things a guy can fantasize about doing that wouldn't be so great in reality."

"Yeah, I've heard that before." Carter sipped the last of his beer then set the bottle on the table. "This Dare's beer is pretty good. It's a local brewery, like Rogelio said. I wonder if they do tours — or if it's made in some guy's bathroom."

"In the bathroom?" Eddie asked, frowning as he picked up his beer. "Why the bathroom?"

Carter chuckled at a fond memory. "I had a friend back in college, he made his own beer for a while. He didn't have all the equipment he needed, so he'd scrub down the bathtub and pour the ingredients in there. The whole apartment smelled like beer. It was crazy, but not too bad until he made the batch that exploded."

Eddie's eyes went wide. "In the bathtub?"

"No," Carter said. "No…in the bottles. It was, er… Well, we didn't get our deposit back from the apartment when we moved out, even though we fixed the wall and ceiling. At least the damage was only to our place."

"Man, tell me this friend of yours didn't go into the beer industry," Eddie mused.

"Actually, he was studying law. I'm not sure what ever happened to him." Carter didn't want to bring a depressing topic up, and admitting that his former friend had severed their friendship over Carter's coming out would likely do that. "He's probably still making explosive beer."

This time they saw Mathias coming over to their table. "Would you like to see the dessert menu?" Mathias asked. "Another beer?"

Carter gave the barest shake of his head.

"No thanks," Eddie answered. "Dinner was excellent and we're both pretty full. Do you know anything about the company that makes this beer? It's damned good stuff."

Mathias preened a little as he picked up Eddie's empty bottle. "All I know is that it's awesome beer. The Pale Ale is my favorite, actually. I'm not man enough for the stout." He grinned and set the bottle back down. "I think the restaurant owner is friends with the guy who makes the beer. Or maybe they're friends now because of it. I'm sorry I'm not being very helpful, but I'd bet you can Google it and find out anything you'd want to know."

"Of course, Google knows all," Carter agreed. "I would seriously be lost without it." He'd look the microbrewery up and see if they did tours. It'd be an interesting date for them to have.

"If you've got the bill ready, I can give you my card," Eddie said.

"And mine," Carter added. He raised a hip so he could remove his wallet from his back pocket. "Here you go," he said to Mathias a moment later, while handing over his credit card.

"This was a nice splurge." Eddie ran the toe of one shoe along the side of Carter's ankle. "It won't be the highlight of this date, however. I want to take you home and fuck you until you scream."

Carter wanted that too, so badly that he had difficulty swallowing around the lust that welled in him. "Me too," he rasped, pressing a palm over his erection. "You're staying with me this weekend, right?"

"I am," Eddie agreed. "That was the plan and I sure as hell am not going to alter it."

"Oh good." Carter didn't know why he was so worried that their budding relationship was going to fall apart. Had he worried so much over previous ones? He didn't think so. Eddie had already come to mean more to him in the short time they'd known each other than had most of Carter's exes. Part of that might have been because Eddie knew and accepted a fact that those exes hadn't been able to.

Carter wanted a polyamorous relationship, an exclusive one wherein he and his partners loved each other and were faithful. That concept had been horrific to any of his exes he'd broached it with, but Eddie was different.

And he gave Carter hope.

Chapter Two

Eddie thought he'd done well hiding his anxiety from Carter. The fact was, they'd met at a bar, connected in a way Eddie had never connected with anyone else, and that connection was still there, strong and sparking between them. They'd met again by chance, and Eddie had thanked his lucky stars for it. Carter had been on his mind constantly from the first time they'd met and there was no sign of that changing.

There was the very real chance that they would make their budding relationship into something strong and enduring. Eddie could feel it in his core. He was aware of Carter's desire to bring another man into their relationship and Eddie was amenable to that, though at this point he couldn't imagine wanting anyone with the same intensity he wanted Carter.

As he drove behind Carter toward Carter's place, Eddie decided to deal with the as-yet unreal third man later. For now, he wanted all of his attention on Carter. There was just something about him that drew

Eddie in. They had a shared love of the outdoors for one thing, which was great.

But there was a shadow in Carter's eyes sometimes that allowed Eddie a glimpse of the man's wounded soul. Eddie knew the backstory of Carter's childhood, growing up with a germaphobe mother who wouldn't let him go outside. He had been homeschooled until his mother collapsed and died when he was seventeen. After that, Eddie could only guess at Carter's past. They hadn't discussed it, but Eddie knew they had time. They would hopefully have the rest of their lives to get to know each other.

Maybe he was pinning too much hope on them, but Eddie didn't see the harm. He wasn't in love with Carter, but he liked him and they burned up the sheets together in bed. With time, Eddie could see himself loving Carter, spending his life with him. It was a goal worth striving for, and if Carter was interested in a future together, Eddie believed they could make it work.

A third man might be problematic. Eddie wasn't the jealous sort—he'd had lovers he'd shared when it was what they both wanted. Rather he wasn't the jealous sort when it was all agreed on and everyone was honest. He despised cheaters and liars, especially since there was no need for such underhandedness when he was open-minded. All he asked was that he could watch and—if he wanted to—participate. Sometimes watching had been enough, but he doubted that would ever be the case with Carter. Eddie simply wanted him too badly.

"All things we need to discuss at some point," Eddie muttered, knowing that saying it out loud would help him better remember to do just that. At least he wasn't making a relationship to-do list on his phone's note app like his brother Chris bragged about doing.

That was probably why Chris was single. Women generally dumped him after a few weeks and while Eddie felt bad for his brother, he also knew Chris was too rigid about some things and he needed to lighten up.

Maybe he'd suggest a threesome to Chris—not with him, because that would be disgusting. Also, Chris was straight.

Eddie quit thinking about his brother as Carter turned into an apartment complex. It appeared to be a newer one, the units modern and the bits of unpaved areas landscaped beautifully. Eddie also noted that none of the vehicles he drove past were junkers, they were all pretty nice. His pickup wasn't a piece of shit, but it was a decade old. It was also paid off and he would hang onto it until it died.

Carter drove back toward the last row of apartments. He parked and Eddie found a spot not too far from him. He shut the engine off then unbuckled. His duffle was in the back seat, and he got it before leaving the vehicle. A click of a button and the truck was locked. Carter strolled over to him and gave him a simmering look that was unmistakable with the way the parking lights illuminated his features.

"I'm glad you're here," Carter said, taking his hand out of his pants pocket. He touched Eddie's arm. "Really glad. I want this to work."

"We'll make it work." Eddie would have loved to have kissed Carter but didn't. He shifted the bag to his other hand. "We're smart guys and successful in our jobs. We can be successful in this, too."

Carter's smile eased a knot of worry Eddie hadn't been aware of until then.

"You're right. Come on. Let me show you my place."

Eddie followed Carter, devouring him visually. Carter was thin but not too much so. He had broad shoulders and long, lean legs. And Eddie knew just how firm and tight Carter's ass was, the way his cum tasted and the sounds he made as he climaxed. He knew the musculature of Carter's thighs and calves, the ripple of his abs as he tensed before shooting his load. Eddie had memorized everything about Carter that he could during their last meet-up, because he hadn't been certain he'd get to see Carter again, despite their connection.

Carter had proved he'd meant it as much as Eddie had. They both called each other every other day at least and texted quite often. Even so, Eddie had feared their attraction wouldn't be as strong when they got together again, but it was.

As soon as Carter opened the apartment door, Eddie crowded behind him, shuffling Carter in bodily. He slammed the door shut behind them and dropped his duffle.

Carter spun around and plastered himself to Eddie. He grabbed at Eddie's arms. "Please."

Like Carter needed to beg, but they both enjoyed him doing it. Eddie pulled Carter even closer, cupping his ass with one hand and his jaw with the other. "Next time, we'll start with this." He kissed Carter, pressing his lips to Carter's firmly and sliding his tongue into the warmth of him.

Carter tasted so good, like strength and need and joy. Eddie wasn't the only one who moaned as he deepened the kiss. He moved his hand from Carter's jaw to the back of his head to better hold onto him. Eddie plundered his mouth, laying claim to every bit of it. He pulled back enough to suck on Carter's bottom lip.

Carter whimpered and thrust his cock over Eddie's thigh.

Eddie squeezed the handful of ass he was holding, making sure he'd leave marks on that taut flesh. Then he added a swat to it, which got a purr out of Carter.

Eddie did it again, the force of the spank driving Carter against him. He clenched the buttock in his hand. "Strip," he ordered. "I want you naked and sucking my dick in a minute flat." It likely wasn't possible, but it'd be fun for them both. He nudged Carter back and let go of him. "Starting now."

"Yes," Carter hissed, toeing out of his shoes. He had his jacket off before the second shoe skidded across the hall.

Eddie went to work on his belt, then his zipper. To his surprise, Carter was nude only seconds after Eddie had freed his own dick. "Suck," Eddie said, holding his cock at the base. "I've beat off every night thinking about your mouth." And the rest of Carter, too, but Eddie didn't say as much because his shaft was encased in wet heat that stole his ability to speak.

Carter palmed his balls while at the same time tonguing his slit.

Eddie framed Carter's face with his hands. "Let me," he asked when Carter glanced up at him.

Carter hummed around his dick and Eddie took that for a yes.

He began to thrust, shallowly at first, not wanting to overpower Carter completely. When Carter mewled and closed his eyes while he sucked harder, Eddie let himself go, pushing his dick in deep until it breached Carter's throat.

"Fuck yeah," Eddie gritted out, his orgasm already too close to occurring. Carter was too good at blowjobs for Eddie to last long or to allow Carter to blow him for more than a few minutes if Eddie wanted to fuck Carter.

Still, Eddie moved one hand to the top of Carter's head. He took a handful of hair and tugged.

Carter didn't protest. Instead he moaned and increased the suction until Eddie could hardly even see straight.

It was as if Carter was as eager for more as Eddie was. That thought was too tempting to resist. Eddie used his grip on Carter's hair to fuck his mouth, controlling the movements of Carter's head. Very few men were able to give up control as thoroughly as Carter did, and Eddie was going to reward him for it. There was no reason to be selfish and deny either of them what they wanted.

Eddie grunted and pumped his hips faster. His legs shook and his breathing was choppy. Warm tingling strands of pleasure began to spread up from his groin and Eddie couldn't hold back. "Coming," he got out as he lost his rhythm. He didn't let up on his grip on Carter's hair.

Carter dove down and swallowed.

Eddie gasped as his cock pulsed. He shuddered with every jet of spunk that shot from his slit, and finally had to tug Carter's head back to get him to let off some of the pressure.

"You're so good at that," he managed to say, offering praise because Carter damn well deserved it. Eddie rolled his head from side to side then opened his eyes and looked at Carter. "Now I'm going to blow your mind."

"I'm so close already, it won't take much," Carter said rather breathlessly. "I love sucking you off. Makes me so hard." He reached down and stroked his dick.

"Don't." Just the one word, but Eddie knew it was enough.

Carter let go of his shaft. "Yes, sir."

Eddie just studied him for a moment, because Carter was so sexy on his knees, his cock hard and glistening with pre-cum. There was enough need in his pretty eyes to make Eddie's gut ache. He wanted to give Carter everything he would ever need or want. "Up," Eddie said. He helped Carter to his feet. "Show me the closest place to bend you over."

"Oh Jesus," Carter mumbled, cheeks tinting pink with a blush. "The sofa?"

"That'll work." Eddie picked up his bag then followed Carter to the living area, which was right around the corner. The couch was white, either leather or the fake stuff. Either way, it was about to get put to excellent use. Eddie caught Carter by the shoulders and guided him to the back of it. "Down you go."

Carter bent until he was draped over the back nicely. "Like this?"

Eddie swatted his pert butt. "Oh yeah."

Since Carter moaned and humped eagerly, Eddie spanked him again. He kept at it until Carter's ass was nice and pink, and Carter was babbling, begging for more. Then Eddie knelt. He pushed Carter's legs farther apart. Carter's balls swung between his thighs. Eddie cupped his sac and gave it a light squeeze.

"Oh," Carter gasped. He arched his lower back. "More."

"What do you say?" Eddie barked out, slapping Carter's buttock harder than he'd yet to do. The skin went dark red after chasing off the white of his handprint.

"Please!" Carter sobbed. "God, please!"

Eddie had a lot to discover about Carter, such as boundaries, but they'd get there. For tonight, he was going to flood Carter with pleasure. Eddie parted Carter's cheeks and buried his face in his crease. One lick, and Eddie was hooked.

He lapped his way down to Carter's pucker. The tight little ring clenched every time Eddie tongued it. He pushed at Carter's cheeks, spreading them further, stretching Carter's hole until it gaped.

Then he began tongue fucking him, shoving his chin against the tender skin between Carter's pucker and balls.

Carter keened and begged for more. Eddie kept licking, giving Carter only his tongue to ride. Occasionally he slapped one of Carter's ass cheeks, and Carter would shudder. Eddie slipped a hand around to fist Carter's dick. It was hard as stone, so hard it had to be painful. Eddie tightened his hold on it and rimmed Carter's ass, curling his tongue to tug at the ring of it.

"Argh!" Carter humped sloppily into his hand. His pucker constricted around Eddie's tongue. Eddie quickly pushed one of his thumbs in beside it and Carter bellowed, hot spunk spurting over Eddie's other hand.

Eddie kept teasing his rim, rubbing his thumb around it as he moved his head back so he could watch what he was doing. God, he wanted to fuck Carter, but he needed a little more time.

After Carter's orgasm ebbed, Eddie withdrew his thumb and started massaging Carter's butt. "Gonna have marks," he warned.

"Good," Carter said in a gruff voice. "I want to feel you for days."

Eddie could do that. God knew he'd feel Carter with him after they parted because the man had sure gotten under his skin.

Chapter Three

Carter was more than pleasantly sore the next morning. He was almost *too* sore. Eddie had fingered him until Carter had come not an hour after bending him over the couch, then he'd woken Carter up and fucked him through the mattress in the middle of the night.

And the morning had started off with shared blow jobs and Eddie once again finger-fucking Carter. Eddie seemed to like ass play as much as Carter did. Add in the occasional swat to Carter's butt, and they were a perfectly matched pair when it came to sex. Carter liked topping on occasion, but he didn't want to fuck Eddie.

There was probably some kind of psychological bullshit theory about that. Carter wanted Eddie to top him, to dominate and control him, even hurt him a little. But he didn't want to do any of that to Eddie in return, though he wasn't averse to rimming or fingering him.

However, Carter would throw down another man and fuck him until they were both too sore to wiggle.

It just wouldn't be Eddie. Nor did Carter want to see anyone else fuck Eddie.

"You only top, right?" Carter asked, unable to keep the question back. Of course he blushed, because he just had to blurt the question out over breakfast. At least they were dining in since he'd made them French toast.

Eddie sputtered on the food he'd just taken a bite of. He covered his mouth while his eyes went wide and started watering.

"Er, bad timing with that, sorry." Carter got up. "I'll get you some water. More coffee too, if you need it."

"Carter," Eddie squeaked out before clearing his throat. "It's fine. I just wasn't expecting you to ask that...then."

Carter got him a glass of water anyway. "Here, just in case I try to kill you with a question again."

Eddie snorted. "Yeah, I'm sure that was your plan, you evil genius."

"That'd be like cutting off my dick to spite my balls," Carter said. "Forget the whole nose saying. I'd be hurting myself more by doing away with you."

That made Eddie grin, and Carter thought there was a blush under that tanned skin of his.

"I'm not sure but that might have been the nicest thing anyone ever said to me." Eddie took a sip of his water then set the glass down. "And to answer your question, I don't particularly like to bottom, no. I tried it a few times. It's just not for me." He shrugged then cast a worried look at Carter. "Will that be a problem? You liked fucking Georgie, so—"

"It's fine," Carter cut in with before Eddie could stress himself about it. "I do like to switch, but it isn't something that I want from you. It wouldn't seem right—" Now it was his turn to shut up. He was in danger of shoving his entire leg in his mouth, not just his stupid foot.

But Eddie didn't seem bothered by the admission. "I'm glad we agree on that. Some guys have told me I'm a selfish prick because I won't bottom, but I know for a fact I hate it, no matter what's done along with it to make it enjoyable. It just isn't for me. So it works out perfectly if you don't need that from me, especially since you've said you want to add another person to this relationship at some point. If you need to fuck someone just to get off like that before then, we can do that together, too."

Carter wasn't sure what to say to that. Was Eddie already wanting to mess around with other people?

Eddie cursed softly. "I can see by your expression that you're on the verge of freaking out. What's going on in your head?"

"Are you going to be okay with it?" Carter asked. He shook his head. "Wait, that's only part of it. Are you...are you going to want to have sex with other guys?"

"Not unless it involves you," Eddie said. "Carter, right now you're all that I want. I'm sorry if that's creepy, but it's the truth. That doesn't mean I'm against bringing someone else in, and I don't mind sharing, as long as I'm not excluded. But I wouldn't be out looking for more."

Carter felt like a selfish bastard. Why couldn't he be happy with Eddie alone?

"Oh now, don't do that." Eddie scooted his chair back then got up. He strode around the table to Carter's side. Eddie squatted and put an arm around Carter. "You sure keep having some worrisome thoughts. Look at me."

Carter did, staring into Eddie's deep black eyes. "I just feel like a selfish jerk. I should be happy with what I've got—and I am."

"Right now, maybe," Eddie agreed. "But you want more, and there's nothing wrong with that when we both think it's okay. I'm fine with it. Right now I'm just so wrapped up in you I can't imagine anyone else catching my attention. I don't think they will unless you point them out, either. What you have to understand is, I'm open-minded as can be. I like fucking you and making you come, and I also like watching you fuck someone else. You taking Georgie, that was beautiful to see. Better than any porn on the 'Net. I don't mind sharing, as long as I know you'll still be mine."

"I will," Carter promised, his pulse racing. "I mean, I don't want to replace you."

"You just want to add to us eventually, and I get that. It's fine." Eddie kissed him, deeply, thoroughly.

Carter had to turn in this chair and hold onto Eddie, because he made Carter's head spin.

"We'll be fine," Eddie assured him a minute or two later. "We need to talk and be honest, and see each other as often as possible."

"I can come out to Big Bend every weekend that you can't get off," Carter said. "I don't mind. You know I love it there anyway."

"Sounds perfect. I'll spend my two days off in Odessa." Eddie arched both eyebrows. "Should I bring my RV?"

"What? No!" Carter lightly thumped Eddie's shoulder. "Don't be silly. We'll get you a key made and you can stay here. It'll be good for us."

"It will." Eddie nuzzled his cheek. "You're good for me."

"Oh, same," Carter whispered as Eddie suckled on his earlobe. Eddie's warm breath over the wet skin made him shiver. "Eddie…"

"Right here." Eddie nipped along his jaw. "I think we should let the anticipation build, though. I want to have you begging me by the time I take you."

"I'm already close," Carter admitted.

Eddie stroked his cheek, then stood up. "That's a start. So, has Mark been giving you any shit at work?"

"Talk about a mood killer," Carter groused. "There was a bruise on his jaw from where you hit him. Not that he said as much, but it was a bruise, and it was there shortly after you decked him."

"Accidentally," Eddie said. "Although, considering how nasty he was to you, I wish I'd have punched him intentionally. Then there'd have been no question about whether or not he was bruised."

Carter chuckled. He could imagine that Eddie would have broken Mark's jaw if he'd wanted to. "Well, he's kept it to glares and sneers for the most part." Carter didn't mention the crude comments Mark had made off the clock a couple of times. There was no reason to upset Eddie. "It still squicks me out that he was a part of your other threesome with Georgie."

Eddie grimaced. "I told you. I didn't fuck Mark. He was such an obnoxious asshole I almost gave up on the whole thing."

Carter sighed. "Yeah, but Georgie was a lot of fun."

"Yeah he was. Not as much fun as you are." Eddie ruffled Carter's hair and laughed when Carter scowled at him.

"Ass," Carter muttered, not that he really minded Eddie messing up his hair.

"If it's not too hot, do you want to hike the Odessa Meteor Crater or Big Spring State Park?" Eddie asked.

"As long as the temperature doesn't hit a hundred or more, I'm game."

"It never gets hotter than that in Big Bend?"

Eddie nodded. "It does, and I don't hike for pleasure then. Just for my job."

Carter got up. "I don't blame you. As much as I want to hike the Appalachian Trail, I couldn't do it in temperatures like we get here. In fact, I'll make sure to begin to hike the AT in late April. There might be snow then, but it beats the heat." Carter sighed dreamily before shaking his head. "Enough of my babbling. Let me clear the table off and load the dishwasher, then we can get ready."

"I'll help." Eddie touched Carter's right hand.

Carter glanced at him.

"It's not babbling," Eddie informed him. "Talking about hiking the Appalachian Trail. Hiking is your passion, and there's nothing to be embarrassed about." He gathered the plates and silverware while Carter took their cups and water glass to the sink.

"Thanks," Carter murmured.

Eddie wasn't certain if he meant for the help or for understanding Carter's love of hiking. He supposed it could be both. "You're welcome."

They worked together in a manner that soothed Carter—not that he was on edge. It was just a sign to him that they fit.

"I've got a backpack all ready to go. Just need to get some water." Carter liked to be prepared.

Less than half an hour later, they were on the road in Eddie's truck. "Where's your motorcycle?" Carter asked him.

"In storage at a co-worker's garage. I'll ride it in on the days I spend here from now on." Eddie gave him a knowing look. "You want a ride on it?"

"I've never been on one before," Carter admitted. "And your motorcycle is really sexy."

"It is. It's a V-Rod Muscle bike." The pride in Eddie's voice couldn't be missed. "I didn't want a typical Harley, and the bike I really wanted was close to thirty grand, which was just too steep. The V-Rod is pretty awesome, though. I'd love to take you out on it."

"It's a date, then." Carter frowned. "Do I need to buy a helmet?"

"I have an extra. I'm a good driver, Carter, but it's not usually the fault of the motorcyclist when there's a wreck. People in cars and trucks don't watch out for us. They only think about other cars and trucks being on the roads, so most motorcycle drivers are damned vigilant drivers," Eddie said.

"I trust you."

Eddie huffed. "Well, it isn't me you have to worry about. Regardless, I'll keep us safe. I wouldn't let anything happen to you."

"You don't have to convince me. I feel safe with you." Carter considered that for a moment. "I think because you accept me."

"Whatever the reason, I'm glad for it." Eddie reached over and patted Carter's leg. "We're going to make this work."

"We will. Can I ask you a personal question?"

Eddie smirked. "More personal than whether or not I bottom?"

Carter almost cringed. "Well considering we've fucked several times, I'm not sure that's really a personal question."

"Ah." Eddie patted him again. "This is where you ask about exes."

"Not all of them," Carter said, figuring he was being perfectly reasonable. "And I don't want details, exactly. I'm just wondering if you had many long-term relationships and if so, what happened. I'll share the same. In fact," he twisted in his seat, hitching one knee up on it to get himself more comfortable. "I'll go first. I've had a few casual relationships, more one night stands than I should have, and two boyfriends I dated for over a year each. Those fell apart because I tried to talk to them about exploring polyamory. They were against it. Then they were against me and wouldn't believe I wasn't going to cheat."

"But you wouldn't have been happy," Eddie pointed out. "If you'd stayed with them, it wouldn't have worked."

"Maybe," Carter conceded, "Or if they hadn't dumped me, I might have been content to remain monogamous with either Ted or Jesse. They didn't give me a chance after that to prove it, so I kept everything else casual after the last big blow up. Jesse was rather indignant about my perversion, as he called it."

"They weren't for you," Eddie said. "And you wouldn't have been happy. You shouldn't have to give up something that you feel you need in order to make someone else happy."

"Neither should they." Carter got it though. "So yeah, we wouldn't have worked out, or I'd have been resentful. I don't know, I felt like I was warped for a good while, but you see more and more on TV and online about polyamory and being monogamish, as Dan Savage terms it. I think that's helped me feel less like a perv and more like a man who simply knows what he wants."

"Nothing wrong with that. I would like to spend some time with it being just me and you before looking for someone else to bring in." Eddie ran the fingers of one hand through his thick hair. "My relationships have generally been short-term ones, mostly because I was in a pattern of dating jerks. Every one of my boyfriends cheated on me and after the last one, I finally decided to stop falling in love on the first date or fuck and trying to build my life around another man's. Now, I know we're moving fast," Eddie said, glancing at him before returning his gaze to the road. "But I can say for certain I'm not in love with you. I like you, sure, and I want us to work, as I've said. I'm not willing to pack up and put in for a transfer or put our name on a lease together—both things I've done in a stupidly short amount of time. I guess I want that happy relationship like my folks have so bad that I just kept trying to rush it. And now I'm not. I'm not willing to let you slip away because I'm too cautious, either, so I'm working on this middle ground we have between us."

Carter scratched his chin. "I think that's the nicest non-declaration of love I've ever gotten," he mused. "I'm not in love with you either, but I could see it happening. I get this warm feeling inside when you call or text me, and seeing you..." Carter waggled his eyebrows when Eddie glanced his way again. "Instant boner, man."

They both laughed and the mood lightened.

The rest of their weekend together sped by too quickly.

"You'll be back on Wednesday?" Carter asked, when Eddie was packing up his bag. There was something he wanted to give Eddie but getting the nerve to do so was proving tricky. Carter toyed with the item in his pants pocket.

"On the bike, yeah, so be prepared. I might even pick you up from work on it." He flashed Carter a wicked grin. "Think about Mark seeing you get on behind me. Might be enough to get him to leave you alone."

Carter canted his head. The thought of riding that motorcycle at all was enough to make his cock perk up. "I'll take a change of clothes. Jeans, boots, leather jacket."

Eddie's smoldering expression was enough to have Carter reaching for him. "You do that," Eddie growled. "And I can leave in an hour instead of now."

"Only an hour?" Carter teased. "That's all I get?"

In minutes Eddie had him laid out on the bed, naked as the day was hot. "You get as long as it takes us," Eddie vowed.

Carter's previous moment of worry over giving Eddie a gift vanished under a wave of lust as he parted his legs, offering Eddie a view of everything. "What're you going to do to me?"

Eddie's wicked grin was the only answer Carter got just then. Eddie climbed onto the bed and rolled Carter onto his belly. The first swat stung, but Carter quickly began to push his ass up to meet each blow. He already had bruises here and there on his backside, and he'd be looking at them every chance he got. Eddie's marks turned him on, and though he'd never admit it to anyone except possibly Eddie, they made him feel owned in a way he wasn't entirely proud of but craved nonetheless.

Eddie didn't prep him. He was spanking Carter one minute, then tearing open a condom the next. "You good with this?" he asked.

Carter rubbed his face on the blanket. "Yeah. Fuck me, please." He was sore but not so much that he couldn't take another round.

Eddie spread lube over his hole. "You're all pink. You sure?"

"Yes," Carter whined. "God, please, get in me!"

Eddie slapped his ass then crawled over him. "Going to cover you, take you like this." He settled his knees beside Carter's thighs framing them.

Carter shivered when he felt the wet tip pressing against his hole. "Aw gawd," he drawled as Eddie thrust, sinking his cock in deep.

Eddie rumbled and lowered himself down until he was almost lying on Carter. He worked his hands then forearms beneath Carter and held onto his shoulder and neck.

It was perfect. Carter felt protected and wanted, a combination he'd never have thought he'd enjoy until he experienced it. He was quickly coming to crave Eddie. That acknowledgment only fueled his arousal, driving him quickly to the edge of climax. He was into Eddie more than just physically. He'd fallen fast and hard for the man.

The emotional involvement intensified everything he felt. Carter moaned and whimpered, squirming and writhing with the impending blissful release. His dick was getting good friction on the sheets. Eddie was driving into him hard and fast, and that made Carter fuck the mattress in return.

Every inch of Carter's skin burned with need, his pulse jetting it to every part of his body. He loved the weight of Eddie on him, the slide of skin, the slap of Eddie's hips against his ass. It was too much and yet not enough. Carter was so close, but he wanted even more.

"Yeah," Eddie panted, "Fuckin' perfect," he added as he slammed into Carter's ass. "Sweet, sweet, ass. Gonna…" Eddie huffed and thrust even more forcefully. The words, combined with the sensation of being stuffed full, sent Carter spiraling from the ability to think to doing nothing but *feeling*.

The next time Eddie rammed in so deep, Carter's orgasm rocketed through him. There was a roaring in Carter's ears that he later understood was Eddie's shout as Eddie came, too.

It was one of the most intense releases Carter had ever experienced in his life. He couldn't even move other than to gasp for several minutes.

"My God," Eddie mumbled. "You're going to kill me. I'm gonna die of pleasure." He slowly pulled his cock from Carter's throbbing ass.

Carter backside was a bit more tender than he'd thought, but that fucking was worth any discomfort he might experience later on — or right then, for that matter.

"I don't want to leave," Eddie said, right before stringing kisses down Carter's nape. "But I have to."

Carter tried to agree. He couldn't get the words out. He almost drifted off to sleep knowing he'd be alone when he woke up, hoping it'd get easier to say goodbye. It was the realization that Eddie would be gone soon that kept Carter's eyes from staying shut.

"Eddie."

Eddie curled over him so that Carter could see his face better.

Carter touched his cheek. "I…I have something for you."

Eddie's eyebrows rose as he murmured, "Oh?"

Carter nodded. He had to move, had to get up and find his pants, dig the gift out of his pocket. It was quite possible that Carter had never been so nervous in his entire life as he clasped the little bit of metal. He squeezed his hand into a tight fist, then Carter walked back to the bed. His entire arm shook as he slowly raised it to offer Eddie this tiny gift that meant so very much.

Eddie sat up on the bed, watching *him*, his face, not his hand. "This is important," Eddie stated quietly.

Carter bobbed his head again, unable to speak past the twin knots of hope and fear trying to strangle him. He unclasped his hand and offered the new key to Eddie. "I-I had t-this made so..." That was as far as he got before his tongue seemed to simply quit working for him.

Eddie glanced down and sucked in a sharp breath when he saw the key. "This is..." He picked it up and curled his fingers around it. Eddie gulped and for a second Carter feared he'd truly fucked up.

But Eddie turned a luminous expression on him, and the smile that spread on Eddie's face was beautiful to behold.

"I love it," Eddie said, "Thank you."

"You're welcome. You're always welcome here." Carter meant it, and he thought Eddie knew he was sincere.

Eddie patted the bed then sprawled onto his back. "Come back here. Lay down with me. Maybe I can be a little late getting back after all."

"I don't want you to be late," Carter said, even as he moved to stretch out beside Eddie.

"Don't worry about it. Let me hold you for a while, okay?" Eddie asked.

It sounded so wonderful, Carter didn't argue. He let them both have what they needed, at least for a little while.

Chapter Four

Carter walked into the restroom and was relieved to find it empty. He didn't feel up to slapping on a friendly smile and conversing with anyone just then. His mind was filled with Eddie and what they'd done together. He was having a little trouble concentrating, which could happen on a slow day at work.

Silently chiding himself to get his head on right, Carter settled on a urinal to use. He unfastened his pants and fished his cock out right as the bathroom door opened. Carter glanced over his shoulder, saw Mark Watson, and just kept from groaning.

Carter had two choices he could immediately see. Take his dick out and pee, or leave and hope his bladder didn't explode on him. Using a stall didn't occur to him until he'd already turned around to leave.

Mark raked him with a contemptuous look and made sure to bump him as he passed. "Running off?" Mark asked.

Carter hesitated but decided it wasn't worth it. He needed his job and wouldn't get in an argument with

Mark over something as stupid as this. He didn't want to argue with Mark at all, yet he wasn't foolish enough to believe he could avoid it forever. He could certainly avoid whipping his dick out in front of the man, though.

"Have a good day," Carter said as he reached for the door.

"Tired of slumming it yet?"

Carter pivoted slightly. "Yes, that's why I'm leaving the restroom now." He put his words into action and was out of the room before Mark's indignant-sounding gasp had finished.

Well, I didn't really argue. I probably should have kept my mouth shut. What if he complains? It wasn't like Mark named anyone off. He could say he was joking and that I harassed him or insulted him. I did insult him. Fuck. Fuck!

Carter worried over the encounter the rest of the day. It made concentrating difficult, and when five o'clock rolled around, he wanted to run for the elevator. He didn't, instead taking the time to go over the last form he'd been working on. He found one mistake and that led him to review everything he'd done that afternoon.

After checking his phone, Carter sent a text to Eddie letting him know he'd be working late. Then Carter got down to it.

"Carter, what are you doing?"

He peered up to find his boss, Becca, standing in the doorway.

"I need to go over these." He tapped the papers. "I was totally scatter-brained today and I'm not going to be able to sleep tonight knowing I might have missed something."

Becca came into his office and stopped beside him. She read over the document in his hand. "I admire your dedication. And I see a mistake on line thirty-six, so I won't try to talk you into going home. We all have bad days, and I'm glad to see you're willing to do what you need to for yours." She started to walk out. "Of course, I'll want to go over all of those tomorrow morning, so leave them on my desk. I'll let security know you'll be here until you finish."

"Thanks." It was embarrassing to have to admit he'd screwed up to Becca, but Carter was an honest man. If she'd chosen to write him up, he wouldn't have blamed her.

Determined to fix his mistake Carter got to work, forcing everything else from his mind. By the time he finished, it was after eight and his back ached from hunching over his desk for hours. He straightened the stack of paper and checked one last time that all the information on the paper copies matched what he'd input into the spreadsheet. Satisfied that he'd done his job correctly, Carter closed his laptop then packed it away in his briefcase.

He took that and the papers with him. Becca's office wasn't locked. Carter waved at the security guard sitting at the desk. "I'm to drop these off on her desk."

"Go ahead." The guard a burly older man named Brandt, watched him while Carter slipped in and out a few seconds later.

"Have a good evening," Carter said.

"You too, Mr. Hausemann."

Carter was a little surprised that Brandt knew his name. Brandt wore a nametag and Carter didn't, and he couldn't recall ever introducing himself to the guard. He shrugged it off. For all he knew, Becca had given Brandt his name.

Carter had worked late a few times and it always felt weird to be standing in the dimmed light of the hallway waiting for the elevator. There were no hushed voices and no need to keep an eye out for Mark. That should have been a relief, yet Carter was on edge when the doors to the elevator opened.

No one was inside. He told himself to get over being so spooked. After he entered the lift, Carter pressed the button for the ground floor. It didn't take long to get there, then he was waving at the front desk security guard there. "Have a good one," he said before exiting the building.

Outside, the dry west Texas air still carried the heat of the day in it. Carter started sweating within three steps. He stopped on the sidewalk and removed his jacket. "Jesus. And it's only April." He'd be cooked on the spot in another month or two if he was outside for long.

The walk to the parking lot seemed to have doubled. Carter was going to have to build up some resistance to the heat or he'd be spending entirely too much time indoors when he wasn't working.

The fear of turning into his mother—or at least of inheriting her mental illness—was always a dark thought hovering in his mind. Carter couldn't stand the idea of that—of not being able to leave his apartment. He'd go crazy if he couldn't be outside.

His car was the only one in the lot, save an older Ford Ranger. He wondered where the other security guards parked and whether the Ranger belonged to any of them.

Then something caught his attention. Since he'd parked two spaces away from one of the post lights in the lot, Carter knew he wasn't mistaken. There was a long scratch down the driver's side of his car. "Someone keyed my—fucking Mark," he growled. There was no one else who would have done it.

Granted, it could have been a random act of violence. Kids, bored and looking for something to do. Maybe he just wanted to blame Mark for it, but Carter couldn't shake the belief he was responsible for the scratch.

Carter touched it. "Oh goddamn it!" It was a deep scratch, not one that could easily be buffed out. He traced the length of it and cursed again. The Jeep was only six months old and he had full coverage insurance — with a deductible that had to be paid. It'd be cheaper than paying for the repair out of pocket.

Disgusted, Carter pulled out his cell phone then called his insurance company. Twenty minutes later, he was finally on his way home. He'd had several texts from Eddie and a missed call by the time he parked in his spot. The first thing Carter did was call Eddie back. "Sorry," he said when Eddie answered. "I miss you, and it's been a shit day and I was driving when you called. How are you?"

"Better now that I'm hearing your voice," Eddie told him.

Carter's heart fluttered and his bad mood lifted a bit.

Eddie continued. "Tell me why your day's been shitty."

Carter strolled to his apartment. "Well, I told you that Mark was limiting himself to the occasional sneer and all. Today he followed me into the restroom. At least, I'm pretty sure he did." As Carter unlocked his door, he filled Eddie in on the happenings, and when he got to the part about the scratch, Eddie cursed louder than Carter had.

"You know it was that bastard," Eddie grumbled. "I should have really decked the fucker just for trying to sneak a peek at your dick. The Jeep, man… That is a low thing to do."

Having Eddie commiserate with him really helped. Carter wasn't even angry anymore by the time he got off the phone with Eddie. He was tired and horny, and really looking forward to Eddie picking him up from work the day after tomorrow.

* * * *

The need to be with Carter was like an itch Eddie couldn't reach to scratch. He kept reminding himself that they were both grown men and Carter didn't need him to come running because someone had keyed his Jeep.

Still, Eddie had never resented his job before. Tuesday dragged by at a snail's pace. Talking to Carter was good, but Eddie needed to hold him in his arms.

Lunch on Weds?

He texted Carter Tuesday afternoon. Eddie didn't want to wait until five pm to see him the following day.

Better yet, breakfast? I can ride out tonight.

Carter texted back within minutes.

You don't have to do that, but I'd love to see you.

That Carter didn't tell him no outright was enough to let Eddie know he needed him too. It wasn't just Eddie falling for Carter, Carter felt the same way about him.

Be there around nine.

After work, Eddie packed some clothes and essentials in the saddlebags and with the Harley gassed up, he was soon on the road. Deer could be a serious and deadly problem on the way, so he made certain to keep a watch out for them. That got trickier when the sun set but the ride was uneventful, and Eddie was parking beside Carter's scratched Jeep a little before nine. He'd made good time.

Eddie unloaded his gear. He'd just started to walk to the apartment when Carter rushed out the door, excitement making his entire face seem to glow.

"I thought that was you," Carter said, beaming at him. "You made it early."

Eddie ached to touch Carter. "Yeah, I had incentive." He held up the spare helmet. "So, about that ride. Are you interested in taking it now?"

"Now?" Carter squeaked.

"Well, I'd like to drop my stuff off first, but after that, yeah." Eddie took a step toward Carter. "And I'd really like to kiss you first."

"Oh. We can... You can definitely do that." Carter held out one hand. "Let me take something."

Eddie handed him the helmet. "It's not fancy, but it's the best quality there is."

"Good to know." Carter took it and they walked to his place.

Eddie waited for the door to be shut, then he set his things down before reaching for Carter. "Come here."

"Like you gotta ask," Carter retorted. "God, I'm glad you're here."

"That fucker bother you today?"

Carter gave the barest shake of his head. "No, but he looked smug as fuck."

Eddie didn't have an answer for that, so he settled for kissing Carter, taking possession of his mouth and tasting him until Carter trembled for him.

It was tempting to forget the ride and instead seduce the sexy man in his arms, but Eddie managed to exercise restraint. He ended the kiss and gently cupped Carter's cheek. "Let's ride."

Carter gave a mock shiver. "Ohhh, say it again, stud."

"I'll show you stud." Eddie popped Carter on the ass. "Now come on. We'll get out for a bit, maybe get a drink for you and a soda for me. Wanna check out The Circle — or that other gay bar?"

Carter grimaced. "I don't want to see Mark, and it'd be my luck he'd be wherever we stopped."

Eddie shrugged. "He won't bother you."

Carter sighed and plucked at his T-shirt. "I'm not really dressed for going out, but I wouldn't mind a drink. How about you take me for a ride then when we get back, you and I can open up the bottle of tequila I've saved for an emergency?"

"Sounds like a plan. I've got the key you gave me. You ready?"

Carter bounced on the balls of his feet, more excited than Eddie had ever seen him. "Yes!"

Eddie chuckled as Carter bolted out the door, helmet in hand. Eddie wasn't far behind him.

"Oh hey!" Carter said when they stopped by the motorcycle. "Remember that microbrewery? Dare's?"

"Yeah, that was good beer. I looked for it out where I'm at but no go. Just the usual big name brands." Eddie had meant to pick some up to take back with him last time he was in Odessa.

"Well, they do tours by appointment and some fancy beer tasting and making classes on the last weekend of every month. If you get another weekend off in the near future, might be fun to go do something there." Carter put the helmet on and began fiddling with the strap.

"Sounds like a plan. I'm off the second weekend in May, then I probably won 't be off for another one until late August." The national parks tended to be pretty busy over the summer months.

"That sucks, but we can deal with it," Carter said. "Plus the scheduled tours might be available in the evenings on weekdays. You should read the bio on the guy that makes the beer. I can't decide if he's mysterious or just weird — or if he had a horrible bio writer."

"Maybe we'll meet him and find out it's a combination of both." Eddie put his helmet on. "Ready to ride?"

Carter tipped his head to one side. "Is that a biker saying?"

Eddie almost laughed, but kept the impulse under control since he knew Carter was serious. "It was actually just a question. Thought you might be nervous."

"Oh, no. I'm excited!" Carter actually clapped his hands in a delightful display of enthusiasm. "I've been looking forward to this since you mentioned it."

"All right. Let me get on, then you get on behind me. One thing, lean into the turns with me. It might seem scary. Do it anyway."

Carter nodded. "I trust you, and I've actually seen motorcyclists doing that."

Eddie got on and Carter followed. He felt perfect pressed against Eddie's back, arms looped around Eddie's waist.

Later, he was sure Carter would need to talk and vent about the damage to his Jeep and Mark being a creep. Eddie would listen and try to keep from making it all worse by hunting Mark down and kicking his ass.

But that would be later. For now, Eddie was content with Carter clinging to him, the heady thrum of the engine, and the vibration of the bike when he gave it some gas.

This was what he and Carter needed for now – the freedom of the open road and the thrill of the ride.

Eddie kept within the speed limit. He wasn't willing to risk Carter's life. He drove out of Odessa, through Midland, toward Colorado City. They didn't go that far, though it was tempting to drive until the bike ran out of gas. Eddie did pull over at a rest area outside of Big Spring. He put the kickstand down and turned the motorcycle off.

Eddie removed his helmet, as did Carter, then Eddie helped Carter off before getting to his feet himself. Carter's hair was a flat mess that made him even more attractive for some reason. Eddie liked the big smile Carter gave him, the joy radiating from him. "You want a bike of your own now?"

Carter plucked at the chin strap. "What about dirt bikes? Don't you think that'd be fun?"

"I've known more people hurt on them than a regular motorcycle, but yeah, if we didn't do any stupid daredevil shit, it'd be cool." He plucked Carter's helmet from his hand then locked it to the bike, doing the same with his afterward. "Thought we could stretch our legs a bit."

Carter looked around. "Too bad it's so crowded. We could – you know – mess around, if it wasn't."

A glance down showed that Carter was sporting a nice semi. Eddie winked at him. "Well, you can save that for when we get to your place. I've got dirty plans for you anyway."

"Oh, good." Carter chuckled and started walking. Eddie followed him past the tables and the restrooms. It was dark behind them, and two people walked their dogs out back, so they weren't alone. They could see the stars better, and that was probably what Carter had been looking for. Eddie remembered the way Carter had stared up at the stars at Big Bend. He remembered Carter's words, too. He didn't want Carter feeling small and inconsequential compared to the vastness of the night sky, so Eddie slipped an arm around his hips and nudged him into darker shadows.

"Just a kiss," Eddie murmured before taking one.

Carter melted against him, a sweet shiver going through him that Eddie could feel. Eddie dipped his tongue past Carter's lips, just enough to get a decent taste of him, then he pulled back, mindful of where they were and the dangers of two men making out in public.

"Thanks," Carter said, touching his lips. "I needed this. All of it. You. I needed you."

"I'm here." But Eddie wondered what would happen the next time Mark pulled some bullshit stunt and he couldn't be there in person for Carter. He'd just have to do everything he could to be there any way possible.

"Tomorrow I have to drop the Jeep off at the body shop. Can you follow me and take me to work?" Carter asked.

More time with Carter was fine with Eddie. "Sure. Are we still doing lunch, too?"

Carter laughed. "I want as much time with you as I can get. That's a yes."

Eddie reluctantly let go of Carter. "This is moving fast, but it feels right."

"I gave you a key to the apartment," Carter pointed out. "It's moved fast from the moment we met, even if I did run off like a coward."

"I was so mad at Mark and frustrated because I thought I'd never see you again. He's lucky I didn't break him in two." Eddie got a little pissed off just thinking about that night. Carter had freaked when he'd found out Mark had been part of a ménage with Eddie and Georgie, though Eddie hadn't fucked Mark. "He was a mistake. I shouldn't have been such a slut that night."

Carter shrugged. "There's nothing wrong with getting laid and honestly, Mark isn't bad looking. It's just his personality that's repulsive. If I didn't know him and was looking for a one-off, I might have done the same thing, as much as it galls me to admit it."

Eddie didn't have anything to say to that. He stood with Carter, both of them staring at the sky for a few minutes.

"Take me home," Carter finally said. "I need you."

"You've got me." It was the truth. Eddie had done what he'd said he wouldn't. He'd fallen fast and hard, deeper than should have been possible. That was a secret Eddie would keep to himself for a while.

The ride back seemed to take longer than it should have, partially due to the fact that Carter kept running his hands up Eddie's thighs to his groin. Eddie's anticipation had already been building, but those kinds of touches only increased it exponentially. By the time he parked the bike, Eddie was ready to fuck Carter the second they got inside the apartment.

But Carter had other plans. "Bed. I want you to feel you all over me."

So Eddie took a long, thorough kiss in the hallway, then he led Carter to the bedroom. Eddie ditched his bag and pulled Carter into his arms.

Carter looked at him with such devotion, Eddie thought he might not be the only one who fell too hard and fast. He didn't ask, because Carter probably wasn't any more ready to admit it than he was.

Eddie settled on soft touches, tender kisses, and gentle persuasion as he removed Carter's clothes. "I want to just..." Eddie nibbled on Carter's lips, then his jaw. He wasn't sure how to articulate what he wanted, which was something sweet and loving instead of the rough way they tended to fuck.

Eddie undressed with Carter watching him hungrily. Carter's dick was long and thick, with a wide slit that Eddie could poke the tip of his tongue into. Heavy balls hung between Carter's leanly muscled thighs, the skin of which was dusted with golden blond hair. Carter's hips were narrow, his stomach toned but not sculpted to the point of insanity. His pectorals were slight and topped with peach nipples that already stood erect.

"Turn around," Eddie asked, memorizing every freckle and mark on Carter's body.

Carter's face turned pink with a blush that quickly spread down to his chest. He turned, giving Eddie an excellent view of his backside—and the marks on it. "You still have a few bruises."

"I know. I'm glad, too. Looking at them made me feel like you were with me," Carter stated quietly as he reached back to touch his bottom.

Eddie would make sure to leave some more before he had to leave, just—*not tonight*. He moved to stand right behind Carter. Eddie slid one arm around his middle and one around his chest.

"Oh," Carter exhaled, leaning against him and bracing his hands on Eddie's hips.

Eddie kissed Carter's nape then began loving on him more intensely. He moved his hands over Carter's body, touching his belly, his hipbones, his chest. Carter's skin was mostly smooth, though in a few places it was dry, like at his elbows and hands.

All of him felt good to Eddie, especially the curve of his ass and the rigid length of his cock. Eddie wanted to do everything to Carter at once, but in that moment, holding Carter was perfect. Eddie nestled his dick between Carter's cheeks and began a slow grind that he could definitely get off to.

At the same time, he dragged one hand up Carter's torso, stopping to tease at a nipple, before returning to his original goal. "Lick it," he said, holding his palm in front of Carter's lips. "Get it wet so I can jack you off."

Carter whimpered slightly and began lapping at Eddie's hand. When Eddie thought it was good enough, he reached down and fisted Carter's length.

"God, yeah," Carter muttered, leaning his head back to rest it on Eddie's shoulder.

Eddie sucked a mark up on Carter's neck while jacking him and rutting into his crack at the same time. The buildup was slow but steady, then Carter shook, his hips jutting as he came. Eddie moved to nip at his shoulder. He pressed against Carter's belly, holding him tight while fucking his crease. Eddie came with a ferocity that rocked him to his bones. He didn't even know exactly when it began because one second he was chasing his release and the next he was thrown into such gripping pleasure he couldn't even breathe.

When he came back to himself, his legs felt weak and his fingers tingled. He realized he was holding onto Carter very tightly. "Sorry," Eddie managed to say.

Carter grunted and patted his hip.

Eddie knew how he felt. Even getting one word out had seemed a monumental task. He shuffled them both onto the bed and let his eyes drift closed. In a few minutes, he'd get up and shower with Carter.

Or maybe they would both sleep. Either way, Eddie was more content than he'd ever been in his life.

Chapter Five

After a month of being in a long-distance relationship, Carter knew he and Eddie could make it work. The key was commitment, which they both had for each other. It may have seemed odd that they still discussed bringing in a third man to complete the relationship, and some—okay, most—people would have thought Carter a scumbag for feeling that need still, but Eddie didn't, and his opinion was the one that mattered.

But Carter wasn't in a hurry to enlarge their little love circle. He figured it would happen when it happened, and probably, if he were honest with himself, it wouldn't ever happen at all. The stories he read online about true polyamorous relationships were few and far between. It seemed best not to focus on it too much, especially when he was happy with Eddie. Carter just couldn't help but want more, and half the time he chided himself for that.

Carter checked his reflection in the restroom mirror. Eddie was coming for lunch today, and Carter wanted to look good. The men's room door was opened and

Carter tensed before reminding himself that Mark wasn't there. Two days after the Jeep incident, as Carter thought of it, Mark had volunteered for an assignment in California. It was temporary, but Carter was hopeful that would change. Mark's sudden departure had sealed it for Carter.

He fully believed Mark had been the one responsible for the damage to his vehicle. There was no way to prove it since there were no security cameras in the parking lot. Regardless, Carter was convinced he was right.

Carter didn't recognize the man who entered, which wasn't unusual. There were plenty of people in the building that he didn't know. They exchanged a perfunctory smile. Carter gave himself one last glance then left the room.

"You seem happy today," Becca noted a few minutes later. "Lunch date with that motorcycle driving guy? He's cute."

Carter just knew he was blushing. For one thing, he'd never discussed his sexuality with anyone at work—but Becca *had* figured it out. She'd asked him if Mark was bothering him back before Carter had met Eddie. Carter hadn't even thought about it then, he'd been too busy trying to avoid Mark, but yeah, Becca knew, and she probably wasn't the only one who'd seen him hoping on the back of Eddie's bike. Maybe he shouldn't be so worried about it. He didn't want to get bashed and was usually pretty cautious.

"I didn't mean to freak you out," Becca said with a noticeable amount of concern.

"You didn't." Carter shook his head when she narrowed her eyes at him. "Seriously. I just—you know—have to be careful, and I wondered who else knew."

Becca crossed her arms over her narrow chest. "If anyone gives you any trouble, let me know. We don't tolerate bigotry here. In case you didn't know it, the owner and his partner were married in Maine about a year ago."

"I didn't know that," Carter admitted.

"Well," Becca huffed. "They don't broadcast it, either, but it's not a secret. It's stupid that they, or anyone else who isn't heterosexual, has to worry about being able to get married or feel the need to keep it quieter than they might like. I'll never understand why marriage equality is an issue for people who can already get married, either." She uncrossed her arms and continued. "Anyway, it's good to see you happy."

"Thanks," Carter replied. "It's good to be happy." He didn't point out that there were other companies in the building, and their employees might not share her attitude. He was probably overthinking it all and worrying over nothing. It wasn't like he was mauling Eddie in public. He even held onto Eddie's shoulders when they rode the motorcycle in the daylight hours.

When Eddie texted him, Carter left for his lunch break. He didn't take his suit jacket, not when it was close to ninety out already. "Hey," he said when Eddie lifted his visor and smiled. "Going to have to start doing this in the Jeep or your truck soon. It's hot."

"It is, and we can use your Jeep. I like it." Eddie handed Carter his helmet.

Carter put it on then got into place behind Eddie. They didn't have far to go. It was four blocks down to their favorite Mexican food place. It looked like a dive on the outside, but the inside was spotlessly clean and the food was cheap and plentiful.

Carter and Eddie seated themselves as was the way it was done at Chile Odessa. They waved off the menus when the waitress came over, instead ordering their favorite dishes and drinks.

"Wish I could have a couple of margaritas," Carter said, leaning back in the booth. "Oh, or one of those pineapple drinks. That'd be perfect."

Eddie groaned. "Aw, now I want one and I have to drive. You at least could sneak into your office and sleep."

Carter laughed at that. "Yeah, right. Becca would have my head."

They enjoyed chatting over little things, and mainly just spending the hour together. When they got up to leave, Carter left the tip while Eddie went to pay the bill. The little restaurant wasn't anything like the fancy one they'd went to on their first date, but Carter loved it.

As he walked past the booths and tables in the front part of the place, he caught a glimpse of someone staring through the front window. Why he noticed in the first place, Carter couldn't say. A group of diners stood up and blocked his view. Carter shrugged the whole thing off. It was probably nothing more than a potential customer checking the place out.

But when he left with Eddie, Carter rubbed at the back of his neck.

Eddie noticed his discomfort immediately. "What's wrong?"

Carter couldn't contain a laugh brought on by embarrassment. "Just me being stupid—"

"That's bullshit," Eddie growled. "You're not stupid at all."

"Silly, then," Carter countered with. "I got the creepy feeling that I'm being watched, and no one would be stalking me."

"Always listen to your instincts." Eddie kept them walking a few more steps before he stopped and exclaimed, "Damn it! I forgot the to-go order!" He turned around and Carter caught on quickly.

"It's fine. We can go back and get it." He pivoted as well and looked in the direction he'd felt like he was being watched from. "No one I recognize," he whispered.

"Same," Eddie said.

Carter sighed loudly. "You know what? Let's forget the to-go order. I can't be late getting back to work."

The short drive ended entirely too soon. "I'll see you when I get home," Carter murmured in Eddie's ear before getting off the Harley.

"I'll have dinner ready."

Carter liked the sound of that, especially since he was certain dinner wouldn't be the first thing Eddie gave him when he walked in.

"I'm counting on it." Carter got off the motorcycle and latched his helmet in place. "Later."

"Later," Eddie agreed.

Carter watched him pull away, and no sooner was Eddie down a block then Carter felt creeped out all over again. He did his best to appear casual when he swept the area visually. There were pedestrians and cars, a bit of a lunchtime rush. Carter couldn't pinpoint the source for his discomfort, and he didn't have time to dwell on it.

The feeling didn't return while he worked or when he left for the day. Carter shrugged it off as him just being weird. He had that familiar flash of fear that he was turning into his mother, growing to fear things he shouldn't.

"I am not," he whispered fiercely to himself as he walked to his door. "I am not going to be like her." And worrying that he would was counterproductive to that, so Carter let it all go. He had a sexy man he was in love with waiting for him inside. Nothing could compare to that.

* * * *

"We could go out," Carter suggested to Eddie after they'd shared a kiss. He paced the room, flicking his thumbs against his forefingers. "I'm a little more energetic than usual, and since this is one of your rare three-days off weeks, why not have a little extra fun?"

Eddie ran a hand down Carter's chest then cupped his balls through his slacks. "Sounds like a plan to me. Dress like a slut. Since it's a Wednesday night, the crowd probably won't be...well, a crowd. I want everyone looking at you and knowing you're mine."

Carter almost giggled at that. "You know I love it when you go all growly like that." And he also loved knowing that Eddie wanted other men to stare at him, to want him. Eddie had said Carter could mess around with other guys as long as Eddie could watch or participate, but Carter didn't want casual with anyone. He had serious with Eddie, and any other man that was invited in would have to be interested in that, too.

That didn't mean Carter wouldn't slut it up clothes-wise and dance with any sexy men who asked. "Are you going to bring me back here and fuck me harder than ever after I dance with handsy guys?"

"I might fuck you there in the club," Eddie rumbled. "Now get dressed." He slapped Carter's ass hard enough to sting. "I'm good like this." Eddie gestured to his tight jeans and tank top.

"You are," Carter purred at him. He darted past Eddie, laughing when he got another swat on the butt.

Carter found his favorite pair of black jeans. They were tight in the right places, but not binding or pinching. He put them on, along with a black mesh top he'd never worn before. It was daring for him, as was the liner he added around his eyes. He wasn't a twink at all. It was simply fun to try new things, and the eye liner along with the shirt were two he'd been saving for a special occasion.

After he'd spiked his hair up, Carter put on his vintage red Doc Martens, then he was ready to go.

The appreciative look Eddie gave him had Carter preening a bit.

"Maybe we should stay here after all," Eddie murmured, pinching Carter's nipples as he spoke. "Goddamn. I didn't even know I liked a guy wearing makeup, but you sure are fucking sexy with that black liner around your eyes. Yeah, we could stay here."

Carter's dick began to firm up as Eddie increased the pressure on his delicate nubs. "Oh, no, I—" Carter left off trying to speak and just hissed, the air leaving his lungs and his eyes trying to close as pain and pleasure tangled in his chest. "Ungh."

Eddie twisted Carter's nipples then released them. "Nipple clamps. We are so getting you some."

"I don't know," Carter hedged, rubbing at his tender tips.

Eddie cupped Carter's dick. "I do." Then he gave that a pinch too.

Carter almost came on the spot.

"I know you, baby," Eddie said in a low voice. "And what I don't know, we're learning together."

That was accurate. Carter was learning that he liked pain, more of it than he'd ever have thought to try, and Eddie was teaching him those lessons. They'd started using paddles. Well, Eddie had used them on him, and Carter was already thinking about other implements he wanted to check out.

Eddie hummed and went back to working Carter's nipples. "These... I like it when they're swollen, hot..." He twisted sharply and Carter came up onto his toes. "Raw."

"Eddie," Carter got out in between panted breaths. "We —"

"Are going out," Eddie finished for him. He plucked at the tips then bent to lick one through Carter's shirt. "We should see about getting these pierced."

"Maybe." Carter was both scared and intrigued by the idea, which he knew meant he'd probably do it, soon. "After the microbrewery tour next Tuesday?" *Yep, there went my mouth running off without my brain's approval.*

Eddie beamed at him. "Sounds good. I'll research piercing options here and in Midland. I doubt there'll be anything out in the Big Bend area — or we could do it this weekend."

Carter rubbed his hands over his own tits. "Man, maybe we should wait until it cools back off? They'll get hot when we're hiking on the weekends."

"Eh, I don't think that's going to be a problem. We hike early, though there was a bobcat sighting a few days ago, so we might have to cut that out for now."

"Bobcat?" Carter frowned. "There's always a risk of them out there."

"And that risk is greater at dusk and dawn," Eddie said patiently. "Plus this one was seen near the Chisos Basin campground, which isn't good at all. We've got a lot of campers coming in for the weekend."

"Was it a reliable sighting?" Carter asked.

Eddie nodded. "Beth and Eric both saw it."

Those were two of the Park Rangers Eddie worked with, so Carter knew the bobcat wasn't a hoax some camper made up for attention. "Well, we better be careful. Then again, we always are."

"True enough, and this conversation's gotten too serious. Let's go have some fun. And if you find someone you're interested in…" Eddie arched a brow at him.

Carter stopped mid-reach for the door. He looked at Eddie. "Are you wanting to fuck someone else?" he asked bluntly.

Eddie laughed at that.

Carter glared.

"No," Eddie finally got out. "No, I told you I get turned on sharing a man with someone else. That hasn't changed just because I'm falling hard for you." Eddie cupped his chin as Carter's jaw dropped. "It's true."

Carter's head spun, probably because his heart was beating double time.

"I don't want you to feel like you have to say anything back, either," Eddie said firmly. "No pressure, sweetheart. Just wanted you to know how I feel, how this is going for me, and now you do. If you ever want to tell me you care a lot about me, I'll be glad of it, but—not tonight," he reiterated. "I wouldn't want to worry over it being something you felt obligated to say."

"I wouldn't," Carter denied. "I get what you're saying and I'll respect it." First thing in the morning, he was telling Eddie how much he was falling in return.

Eddie let go of his chin. "Well, all right then. Get that sweet ass out to the bike."

It didn't surprise Carter to see that The Circle had a decent crowd after all. "We aren't the only ones with the middle of the week blues," he noted as they entered the bar.

"Guess not." Eddie put a hand on the small of Carter's back.

The possessiveness of the touch seemed contrary to Eddie's willingness to let him fool around, but Carter got it. He was Eddie's no matter who else wanted him. Carter was good with that.

They didn't get more than a dozen feet inside before Carter pointed out Georgie dancing with a burly looking man who had hold of Georgie by the hips. "Looks like he's found someone to play with."

Eddie grunted and they made their way to a small table set away from the dance floor. The DJ was mediocre, but no one seemed to care as men danced and groped each other under the tawdry flashing lights.

Carter craved a good drink. "I'm going to get a frozen margarita. Want one?"

"I'm going to have one beer but that's it," Eddie told him. "I bet they don't have anything other than the big brands. I'll get our drinks."

Eddie was right, Carter saw, when he returned from the bar with a bottle of Bud in hand, along with Carter's margarita.

"Thanks." Carter took the drink and hummed happily as he sipped at it. "This is surprisingly good. I usually just have a beer when I'm out. Tonight's an exception."

"Bartender said it'd be the best one you ever had," Eddie replied doubtfully.

Carter shrugged. "It's not, but it isn't anything to pour out either. I just expected it to be bitter or watered down."

Eddie took a pull from his beer.

Carter watched the way Eddie's Adam's apple bobbed. It made Carter's dick twitch and his mind shoot straight to the image of Eddie's lips wrapped around his cock.

Eddie smirked at him and set the bottle down. "You should dance."

"With you?" Carter asked.

"Eventually, but not right now. I don't want to leave our drinks, and I really want to see you out there grinding." Eddie's smoldering gaze made Carter's throat go dry with lust.

He took another longer drink of his margarita, making sure he got a good dose of salt from the rim, then he set the glass down. "All right. I'll give you a show, since that's what you want."

"And you don't?" Eddie retorted, quirking a brow at him.

Carter stood and gave what he hoped was a seductive grin. "Oh, I do. I want to see you sitting there, squirming because your dick's so hard from watching me with someone else. I want you ready to bend me over and fuck me because we're both primed for it." He leaned over the table and whispered in Eddie's ear. "I want you to cover me with your scent, with your sweat and cum so that any other man's touch and smell is gone from my body and memory. Think you can do that?" Carter nipped Eddie's ear then backed away as he stood upright. He didn't wait for an answer either, turning and working his way into the writhing dancers closest to him.

Of course Georgie found him right away, and the big man Georgie had been dancing with was still holding onto Georgie's hips like he was afraid he would get away or something.

"Carter! Oh my God!" Georgie squealed, managing to extricate himself from his grabby friend. He caught Carter by the arm and pulled him to the less crowded edge of the dance floor. "I'm so glad to see you—you're wearing guyliner? You are—and damn, you wear it well. Did you hear about the fight with Eddie and Mark?"

Since they had to practically yell to be heard over the music, Carter settled for bobbing his head and pointing Eddie's way.

Georgie's stunned expression was funny to see. He gawped at Eddie, who waved. "You're here with him?"

"We've been seeing each other since we met, or just about," Carter informed him, happy as he could be about that fact. "I… We're pretty serious, I think."

Georgie frowned. "Well, shit. I guess that means you don't want to fuck with me and Gregg—"

"Fred," the big man behind Georgie rumbled.

"Fred, right." Georgie rolled his eyes. "Like the name matters, dude," he muttered.

Carter didn't think Eddie would mind if he did, as long as Eddie could watch, but Carter wasn't looking to fuck around just to get off. "Sorry, Georgie. I wouldn't mind at all if it was going to lead to more, but since it won't…"

"Ugh." Georgie actually stomped one foot. "All you guys are doing the monogamy thing."

"Not exactly. I just said I'm not interested in casual sex now."

Georgie looked at him as if he was insane. "You're talking about having a long-term ménage or...or more. God, what a nightmare that would be." He shuddered, and Carter wasn't sure it was faked.

"My brother's been in one for goin' on eight years, him and another man and a woman. They're as happy as any couples I ever seen."

Carter and Georgie both stared at Fred.

Fred might have smiled but it was hard to tell with all the facial hair. "It's true. Our folks about shit bricks for the first couple of years, then the babies started coming along and Mom and Dad decided they could live with Terry's kinks since it meant the only grandkids they'd ever get. I don't want no rug rats."

Georgie turned to him. "Well, don't worry, Daddy. What we're going to do won't make any."

Carter cringed inwardly at the 'Daddy' endearment, or whatever it was. That wasn't any kind of play he was interested in for sure.

Fred all but lifted Georgie off his feet, hooking an arm under Georgie's butt and bringing him to his toes. "We done here?"

Georgie slithered against him.

Fred picked him up the rest of the way for a few seconds while kissing him ardently. Carter was surprised he couldn't hear slurping sounds from the two of them.

When the kiss ended, Fred put Georgie down and grabbed his ass. Georgie wiggled it then gave Carter a little finger wave. "Catch ya later."

"Sure, I guess," Carter muttered to their backs.

"Wanna dance?"

Carter pivoted and found himself the recipient of an eager, green-eyed gaze. The man asking was probably not conventionally handsome, with a long, pointed nose and thinnish lips. His eyes, though, those were what snagged a guy's attention. They were large and slightly up-tilted, with a ridiculously thick fringe of light-tipped dark lashes framing them. He knew those eyes were green because the strobe had hit them almost as soon as he'd turned around.

"Sure," Carter said, aware that he'd been staring at the man. "I'm Carter."

"Brian. You're really cute."

"Thanks." Carter suddenly felt entirely too old to be dancing with Brian. Anyone who described him as cute was surely hovering around barely legal.

But he noted the faint lines around the outer edges of Brian's eyes and told himself to lighten up and put on a show for Eddie. But he didn't want to give Brian the wrong idea.

Carter nodded toward Eddie. "Just so you know, I came here with him, and that's who I'm leaving with."

Brian glanced at Eddie. "He's pretty fuckable. I don't blame you. Sucks for me, though."

"I'll understand if you don't want to dance."

Brian grabbed Carter's hand. "Uh, no, I do. I'm disappointed, not stupid."

Carter laughed as he moved closer to Brian. "Well, all right then."

Brian was almost as good a dancer as Carter was. They wasted no time moving together. Carter liked the way Brian pressed against him, eager and wiry-bodied, clutching at the back of Carter's waistband.

"He doesn't mind this?" Brian asked a few minutes later when Carter slid one of his legs between Brian's.

"Turns him on," Carter said. "Look at him."

Carter had gotten glimpses of Eddie, enough to recognize the familiar lustful expression darkening his features.

"Oh, kinky, huh?" Brian moved his hands down to rest them on Carter's ass. "This okay, then?"

Since Eddie looked like he was getting off on the show, Carter nodded. Hell, he was enjoying it, too. He tugged on Brian's hips, encouraging him to rut.

"I—" Brian's breath sputtered as he frotted. "Can I—? It's—"

Carter saw Eddie nod. Whether Eddie knew what was going on with Brian, or he was just letting Carter know it was all good, the gesture reassured Carter. "Yeah, yeah he's going to fuck me so hard when we leave here."

"Oh God," Brian whimpered. "I'm gonna—"

Since he was humping Carter's leg like a jockey riding for the Kentucky Derby, Carter understood. He grunted and pressed his leg up harder.

Brian yelped, but not from pain. His mouth dropped open and he trembled while rubbing his groin over Carter's thigh. When Brian finally stopped riding him, Carter patted his butt lightly. "Better go clean up before you get stuck to your jeans."

"When you said that," Brian rasped, chest heaving. "I wasn't counting on getting off, but damn."

Carter felt a little smug about that. "Well, I'm glad you enjoyed it. I did too."

"You came?" Brian asked, darting a glance downward.

"No, but I'll be thinking about this when I do." More like he'd be thinking about Eddie watching them, the hungry, near-primal look he'd given Carter as Brian came undone.

"Wow. Okay. Yeah." Brian was a little wobbly but he shook his arms out and giggled before covering his mouth. He uncovered it almost immediately. "Oh. Not supposed to do that. Guys hate it."

Carter clucked his tongue. He doubted Brian heard it, and what he wanted to say was important so he made sure he was close to Brian. "Fuck that. You be you, Brian. You're pretty adorable, giggles and all."

He wasn't sure but he thought Brian's blushed. "Thanks," Brian said. "Er…for everything." He darted off and Carter watched him for a second before another man stepped in front of him.

"So do I get off if I dance with you?"

Carter didn't like this guy at all. He seemed smarmy, much like Mark was, whereas Brian had appeared to be sincere. "Nah, I'm done."

The man rolled his eyes. "Whatev. You're too old for eyeliner, asshole."

Carter bristled until he recalled the need in Eddie's eyes. "Whatev. I've got him," Carter pointed to Eddie. *And you've got your hand, punk.* Carter kept that snarky comment to himself as he made his way toward Eddie.

"That was fucking amazing," Eddie said, as soon as Carter was near enough to hear him.

"Yeah?" Carter sat down and eyed his margarita. It'd melted some, but not fully. "You know he came."

"Don't blame him at all. I almost did, too." Eddie palmed Carter's balls under the table.

Carter startled then spread his legs wider. "Feels good."

"Drink," Eddie ordered. "Have another one. Dance with some other guys if you want."

Carter licked the remainder of the salt off the rim, knowing Eddie was watching him and enjoying the show. "I'd really like to go home and have you fuck me now."

Eddie squeezed, applying pressure to Carter's balls. "Whatever you want."

Carter chugged the rest of his margarita, getting a mild case of brain freeze from it. "I want you to fuck me."

Eddie's smile had a little bit of a sadistic twist to it. "I will, after I make you beg for it."

"I'm ready to beg now," Carter said, pushing his glass aside.

"Nah, you just think you are. You have *no* idea."

Carter's insides quivered with hot jolts of lust. "Then show me."

Chapter Six

Eddie was still thinking about how he'd done just that on Saturday as he gave a camper a lecture. Eddie had done it often enough now that he didn't have to give his words much consideration. The border between Texas and Mexico was on the murky side for most park visitors. There were not barbed-wire fences keeping people from crossing over to the States.

Sometimes people came over illegally from Mexico. They would leave crafts they had made in the hopes that park visitors would drop money in the jars left there for that reason. Some of the crafts were damned pretty, too, but it was against the law to take them or give money to their makers. It was illegal trade and could result in serious trouble for the American citizen caught doing it.

Didn't stop a lot of them.

Eddie continued on with his lecture until he thought maybe he'd gotten through. He left that campsite and got in his Park Ranger truck. He'd left Carter sleeping in the RV after a vigorous round of sex that morning. Eddie decided it was time to talk to Carter about ditching the condoms when they were with each other. He was sure Carter wouldn't fuck around behind his back. Carter was an honorable man, and so was Eddie.

Plus, while Carter needed a third man in the relationship to feel complete, he wasn't interested in having sex just to get off, not unless it was with Eddie.

That in itself had relieved Eddie when he hadn't suspected it would bother him. He'd certainly enjoyed watching Carter dance with and get off the guy at the bar. Eddie had thought, since he'd been cheated on before, that as long as he was involved, as long as he could at least watch, he wouldn't mind Carter screwing around.

But now he knew it was more complicated than that. He'd been ready to fuck Carter six ways to Sunday when they'd gotten back to the apartment that night. The sex had been scorching, with Eddie pushing more and more fingers into Carter's ass, spreading him open wider than anyone else ever had. He knew so because Carter had babbled it right before coming all over the place. Then Eddie had taken his time fucking Carter, plowing that loosened hole until his head had spun and his balls had drained a load.

There was something even better that had happened afterward. Eddie had no trouble acknowledging how much it meant to be able to sleep with Carter snuggled against him all night. Eddie did have a few niggling worries he hadn't before. He knew Carter still wanted to bring another man in, have him be as fully invested in the relationship as they were.

Eddie was worried he might not be able to watch another man fuck Carter, or —*and*—wouldn't be able to care for anyone even close to the way he cared for —*loved*—Carter. Was he just borrowing trouble, questioning those things? Eddie kept trying to figure that out but hadn't been successful doing so yet.

What he did know, without a doubt—he loved Carter, and making him happy was one of the top priorities in Eddie's life.

"Guess that really answers the questions." Eddie drove along the park road while he considered that. He wasn't stupid. If he couldn't truly be open and accepting of Carter's needs, he'd grow resentful. That would sure as shit kill their relationship.

Nothing had to be decided at that instant, so Eddie let it go for a while. He stopped speeders and people hiking where they weren't supposed to. He was patient and answered inane questions, ignored flirting, and did his job well. Carter knew he might not be able to meet up for lunch. Eddie was hopeful, but it didn't pan out. Instead he found himself heading to the Chisos Basin campground again because someone had reportedly spotted the bobcat.

Eddie doubted the camper had seen the bobcat. It was the wrong time of day for the cat to be out, and especially so close to humans. If the animal had been there, then chances were it was ill. It went against such a critter's nature to be near noisy, stinky people.

After he parked at the campsite, Eddie spent twenty minutes talking to a young man who swore he saw the cat. Eddie couldn't find tracks, no matter how intensely he searched.

"It was right fucking there," the kid claimed.

He was only nineteen and his name was Lem, and Eddie wasn't certain that he was all there upstairs—or that he wasn't messed up on something. He didn't smell like pot, either. Eddie would really rather deal with a pothead than someone high on some other drug. Generally. He supposed there were always exceptions.

"My girlfriend thinks you're hot."

Eddie stopped studying the ground and looked up from where he'd squatted. The belligerent tilt to the kid's chin would have unnerved him, except for the fact that Eddie knew he could break Lem in half without batting an eye. "I'm not interested, and I'm not available," he said flatly. Fuck the kid's pride. Eddie had a job to do. "Calling in a false report can get you in trouble, Lem."

"It isn't a false report," Lem said in a sullen tone. "Isn't my fault you can't find the tracks."

Eddie sighed and stood up. "I'm going to have a couple of other rangers come out here to help me." He brushed past Lem, irritated to no end by the idiot. Eddie was certain Lem's unfounded jealousy had just cost him precious time with Carter.

Searching for the bobcat tracks took the rest of Eddie's day. They did find tracks, older ones a good hundred yards away from the furthest campsite. That was still a danger park visitors needed to be aware of. There were signs posted all over but people tended not to pay attention to them. *Bad shit always happens to other people.*

* * * *

"We get four six-ounce beers, a souvenir stein, and a food pairing afterwards," Carter said, while they waited outside for the taxi. Neither were up to driving tonight. "This is going to be fun."

"It will," Eddie agreed. He shivered, an odd feeling coming over him. Beside him, Carter went very still, gazing out into the darkness on the left side of the lot.

"What is it?" Eddie asked quietly, straining to see what Carter might be looking at.

"That weird sensation of being watched again," Carter murmured, his voice barely more than breath itself.

Eddie stood up a little straighter. "That way?"

Carter grabbed his wrist. "No, don't. I'm probably just being st—"

Eddie growled.

"Silly," Carter finished with, his lips curling up in the tiniest smile. "Mark is still in California. No one else would be fixated on me. It's just my nervous system having a little awkward moment."

"I can still go check." Eddie gently disengaged his arm from Carter's grip. "Won't hurt anything since you're sure no one's there."

Carter narrowed his eyes at Eddie. "You say that like you think I'm lying."

Eddie cursed and stopped himself from storming across the parking lot. "That's not how I meant it." He touched Carter's cheek, a brief caress, then lowered his hand. "I didn't mean it that way at all. I was just trying to make sure you didn't worry about me going over there. Honey." Eddie wanted to hold Carter so badly he trembled inside with the need. "You've felt that way a few times now. Maybe it *does* mean something. Could be someone other than Mark who wants you. It happens to people all the time, some weird fucker sees them and *bam*, they got themselves a stalker. Or it could be a bigoted, twisted asshole who needs his balls handed to him. I don't think you lied," he reiterated, "but I do think you need to trust your instincts on this."

Carter stared at him for a long moment, then the anger he'd puffed up with so quickly left him and his shoulders slumped. "Okay. I still don't want you to go over there then because I felt like something really bad, someone who really wants to hurt me, was over there."

"Was?" Eddie glared in the direction Carter had been transfixed by.

"I don't feel it anymore, and you tell me to trust my instincts, but I feel like an idiot." Carter held up a hand before Eddie could speak. "I'm not an idiot. I've never had premonitions and I don't believe in all that psychic stuff anyway. Trusting my instincts is something I've done in regards to hiking and choosing one trail over another at times. This…" He huffed and shoved his hands into the front pockets of his jeans. "It's just messed up, and I don't know what to believe, other than our taxi is pulling in. I just want to forget this."

"For now," Eddie agreed. "Tell me this first. Have you asked anyone if Mark is still in California? Or are you assuming that?"

Carter scowled.

Eddie figured he had his answer. "Might want to ask Becca."

"I will. I promise." Carter waved at the cabbie.

Eddie didn't tease Carter, but he wanted to. The cabbie had to have figured they were his fare since they were standing outside on the walkway. No one else was out. Eddie let Carter get in first. After he took his seat and shut the door, he confirmed the location with the driver.

"Why do cabs all smell weird?" Carter mumbled.

After peeking to make sure they weren't being eavesdropped on, Eddie offered his theory. "Too much BO, too little cleaning."

"Gross. Shoulda brought Lysol wipes for the seats and handles." As soon as Carter said it, he appeared to be both mortified and panicked. "Shit. I was just joking. I didn't mean—"

"I know you were joking. It's fine. You aren't turning into a germaphobe," Eddie assured him. "Although the wipes might not have been a bad idea."

He could see Carter's relief in the softening of his mouth, the way he stopped pursing his lips like he was trying to hold every word and thought inside.

"You're right. I'm feeling off tonight, I guess," Carter offered. "The thing outside, the germs."

"We're going to forget about everything but enjoying ourselves." Eddie would see to it that Carter relaxed and slowed down the apprehension that kept gnawing at him.

It was a short ride to the Microbrewery. "Have fun," the cabbie called out as Eddie was shutting the door.

"Let's do as the man says." Eddie winked at Carter. "Then I have the name of an excellent piercing shop."

Carter stared at him and seemed to stop breathing.

Eddie rubbed his hands over Carter's chest, pushing hard over his nipples. "Did you think I forgot?"

"N-no," Carter stuttered, something Eddie hadn't heard him do before.

Carter's nervousness fueled Eddie's horniness in some weird-ass circle he couldn't comprehend the why or how of. At least Carter was nervous in a good way, judging by the bulge forming at his groin. His little nipples were erect, too. Eddie liked keeping his man on the edge. He pinched each tit then left off teasing Carter—for the most part. "You have the tickets, right?"

"Me? No you—" Carter stopped and groaned. "You have them, right? You're messing with me."

"Not like I really want to. That would involve a lot more nudity. Like total nudity." Well, now Eddie was going to have to will away an erection.

"Think of Congress," Carter suggested wryly.

Eddie frowned. "Now I have heartburn."

"Ha ha." Carter took a deep breath, released it. "Ready?"

"Close enough." He wouldn't be walking into the building with a noticeable bulge, he hoped.

Of course, Carter walked in front of him and Eddie got to eyeing the nice sway of his ass. It wasn't overly done, but a good, steady stride and Carter's ass flexed with every step.

Carter smirked at him at the door. "Still good to go?"

Eddie growled and untucked his shirt.

Carter chuckled and knocked. Since the tour was a private one, the facility wasn't open. They were getting a fancy technical tour that cost a tidy sum but would be, Eddie hoped, well worth it.

The door was opened.

"Welcome to Dare's," a pleasant-looking older woman said to them. She had a genuine smile, short white hair, and rouged cheeks, or maybe she really had what Eddie's grandma called peaches and cream skin. "I'm Dee, Dare's mother, and you two must be Carter and Eddie. Which is who, or who is who?"

"Eddie here." He waved.

Dee shook his hand then offered hers to Carter. "So that makes you Carter. Dare will be here shortly. We hope you enjoy the technical tour. Dare's been wanting to try them out for a while now, but he's been so busy since the brewery was nominated for a James Beard Award for best wine, spirits, or beer professional. Why, Dare's—"

A warm, robust chuckle preceded the entrance of a man who had to be a few years older than Eddie. He was slight of build, and the clothes he wore looked to be a size or two too big for him. As he neared, Eddie noted the flecks of gray in the hair by his temples.

The new arrival offered a radiant smile, along with a handshake when he stopped beside Dee. "My mom will brag about me for hours if you let her. I'm Dare Habrock. Welcome to my brewery."

Eddie liked him. He seemed genuinely nice and had a good handshake. Dare had finely sculpted cheekbones and a perfectly straight nose that was neither too long nor too short. It tipped up slightly at the end, giving him a more youthful air than his graying hair did. Eddie couldn't tell up close if Dare was older or younger now.

"You make some great beer," Eddie offered, before releasing Dare's hand.

Carter stepped in then. "Yeah, you do. Eddie prefers the stout but I love the Pale Ale. This place is pretty cool inside so far."

"Thanks. I'm glad y'all like the beer. Maybe you can sample some of the new ones I'm considering selling. They're different—flavored beers, which seem to be all the rage in some places. Of course, we're in Texas, not New York, so it might get me hanged." He tittered and Eddie thought Dare was possibly a little nervous, which seemed odd.

Well, for all he knew, Dare didn't usually do the tours. *Hadn't Dee said these technical tours were just starting up? Yup, she did.*

Eddie checked the interior of the front part of the building out. It was basically a large warehouse with high walls that weren't closed off with a traditional roof. Eddie could see the beams and wiring for the lights and such running above their heads. The walls were paneled with a light colored wood grain that warmed the interior up nicely. The floor itself was gray concrete, but glossy as if it'd been sealed professionally.

One the walls were dozens of framed pictures, newspaper articles, and awards. Eddie would bet Dee had hung up most of them. Even now as Dare spoke to Carter, Dee was smiling at her son as if he were the Second Coming.

"Shall we begin?" Dare asked a moment later. Dee sat at her desk and began humming.

Eddie met his gaze and nodded. "Sure." Dare had pretty eyes, the color a soft glassy green. He had a small mouth with a full, finely bowed top lip. Eddie felt a nudge to his ribs and realized he'd been checking the man out. "Sorry," he murmured in Carter's ear.

Carter patted his hip. "We're good."

Dare watched them both, his cheeks darkening with a blush. "Erm. Right this way."

Eddie could see that he'd made Dare uncomfortable and felt like an ass. "Sorry, man. I didn't mean anything by it." He supposed they'd find out right quick if Dare was a bigot.

Dare's blush deepened. "It's...um. Well, it's fine if your..." He darted a nervous glance at Carter.

"Boyfriend," Eddie said at the same time as Carter.

Dare gulped and bobbed his head. "Yes, if your boyfriend isn't going to deck me."

Carter huffed out a laugh. "It's cool."

"I am sorry," Eddie repeated. "I didn't mean to make you uncomfortable."

Dare actually fanned himself then but didn't reply to Eddie's remark other than to say, "Thank you. If you'll follow me?" He hesitated then turned and took a few steps away.

Eddie and Carter exchanged glances, with Carter waggling his eyebrows. Eddie winked and wondered if Carter was trying to tell him something. They quit goofing around and followed Dare.

He really was thin, Eddie decided. He could see the sharp lines of his shoulder blades under his shirt.

"I started this microbrewery in my home over nine years ago," Dare began, pausing to wait for them to join him instead of walk behind him. "Most of this isn't in the bio Mom wrote for the website. I like to share the personal details face to face, if at all. But anyway, I'd been working at a desk job in marketing, and was miserable. I had one passion that made life enjoyable." For some reason, he blushed again. "I began experimenting with different ways to make beer as a means of relaxing and soon after, discovered something that made me decide to live for the moment."

Eddie canted his head. He could tell Carter was listening as intently as he was.

"I was diagnosed with cancer," Dare told them. "Testicular cancer, to be exact."

Eddie grimaced in sympathy, even as he experienced a spurt of fear. His grandparents on his mom's side had both died of cancer, as had one of his uncles. "That had to be terrifying."

"To put it mildly," Dare agreed. "It brought my mother and I closer, since we'd had an, ah, disagreement for several years, so two good things actually came from it. A wonderful relationship with my mother, and this." He waved at the brewery.

"I'd never have guessed your mom and you haven't always been tight," Carter said, echoing Eddie's thoughts. "She seems like a great lady."

Dare looked down at the floor or perhaps his feet, then up at Carter. "Well, you know. Some of the older generation have trouble accepting us, even if there's a health scare like mine."

Eddie came close to grinning but it wasn't appropriate so he held it back. "It's not always just the older generation. My folks and grandparents were fine with it after the initial shock when I came out. I have some cousins that are total fuckheads about it though." He shrugged. "Their loss."

"It is," Carter agreed, taking Eddie's hand in his. "My mom died before I figured out I was gay. I led a pretty sheltered life until she passed. She was the only family I had, so I didn't really have to deal with anything like that. I'm glad your mom came around, man."

"Me too." Dare pushed a hank of hair back from his brow. "So do your monthly exams, guys. That's the message there. Now, on to the brewery. I eventually had to move in with Mom because the chemo really made me sick. I know how lucky I am that I—" He coughed and Eddie wondered what he'd been about to say.

"The company I worked for downsized drastically and I, along with several other people, lost my job. It was a bad time, a bad time indeed. Mom was the one who actually suggested this, starting my own microbrewery, and she invested in it to help make it happen. She knew brewing was something I could do that didn't stress me out and on top of that, I was good at it." Dare walked over to nicely polished wooden bar. "This is our tasting room. Would you like to start out with your preferred beer?"

There were several wooden tables that Eddie thought had been handmade out of mesquite, and some that were most likely made from pine. Each had a chalkboard surface for part of the tabletop and pieces of colored chalk were laid out on them, along with erasers. For some reason, it made Eddie smile. "What are the experimental ones?" Eddie asked.

"Can we write on the chalkboards?" Carter sounded as eager as a kid. "That's a cool idea."

"I thought it added a bit of fun to the whole tour experience and yes, have at it." Dare flicked his hand at the bar. "There's one running the length of the bar here."

Carter hopped on a stool and Eddie followed. He got a kick out of watching Carter doodle while Dare described the new beers.

Eddie gave an apologetic shrug when he finished. "I'm a pretty simple man. I hate to be a stick in the mud, but I'll have the Stout."

"I'll have brewer's choice." Carter smiled at Dare. "Whatever you want to try out on me, I'm game."

The double entendre might have been intentional. Dare coughed and hustled over to get behind the bar. "These aren't your souvenir glasses, of course. You get those when y'all are done, so you don't have to lug them around. Um."

Eddie spotted the trembling in Dare's hands before he turned away.

Carter nudged him and tapped the chalk against the writing surface.

Eddie looked down and read, *I like him. Do you?*

It was so much like a grade-school thing that Eddie couldn't help but be amused. He understood why

Carter was asking though, and doing so in a way that wouldn't add to Dare's obvious jitters

Eddie wrote back. *Yeah, maybe, but I can't tell if he's turned on or freaked out.*

Dare had been chattering while Eddie and Carter had their silent conversation, each erasing the words almost as soon as they'd written them. It was the sudden silence that had Eddie's pulse skipping, because he just knew they'd been busted.

But when he checked, Dare was faced away from them, fussing with bottle opener. "Never freakin' works when I try it."

Eddie leaned over the bar, careful to avoid chalk dust. "What's the problem?"

Dare pivoted around and set a glass of beer in front of Eddie. "It's this stupid opener. I was happy with the plain old cheap dollar one we've always used, but Mitt, the head bartender and tour guide, thought we should have something *spectacular.*" Dare held up what looked to be a failed attempt at modern sculpture.

"What the hell is that supposed to be?" he asked.

Carter leaned over too. "It looks like something made by Chuey Grimes. He's a local artist who recycles trash into usable art."

Eddie and Dare both blinked at that.

"Well, okay, it still looks like trash, but that's what his line is, recycling it into—" Carter sighed. "Okay, more trash that apparently isn't so useful. Can I see the opener?"

Dare handed it over. Eddie sat back and peered at it. "Are you using—which end?" He couldn't tell where the actual opener was supposed to be in the mass of tangled wires.

"The middle, actually." Dare reached over the bar and turned the opener over. Eddie noted the brush of Dare's hands against Carter's. He thought it was accidental, but he knew Carter. He'd tensed beside Eddie, not with indignation but with arousal.

Eddie was going to grill Carter over that later. *Was there a zing of attraction when they touched?* Just wondering about it made Eddie's cock twitch.

"I think that's where your problem is," he said when Carter and Dare remained quiet. Eddie took the utensil in hand and turned it over. "Pretty sure that's not the opener part."

"Well what is, then?" Dare asked. "God, I'm going to Walmart tomorrow and buying a dozen cheap openers. Mitt can deal with it."

"Or he could add some sparklies to them," Carter suggested. "Not glitter, because it would get everywhere, but those colored rhinestones and stuff like that."

"That's a good idea," Dare said, sounding very sincere. "Then he's got his *special* and more importantly, functional bottle opener."

"This seems to be the part you need." Eddie poked his finger between two of the thicker wires. "Maybe. If you wedge the bottle cap in here—can I see the bottle?"

"Sure." Dare got it and handed it over.

Eddie wiggled the cap where he thought it should go. It took him almost a solid minute. "That's ridiculous. Can't have customers waiting that long." A tip of his hand and the cap popped right off. "If that ain't where it goes, then I don't have a clue where the right spot is. I'd throw that damn thing away or hang it on the wall in the storage room if you don't wanna toss art."

That got him one of those nice, genuine laughs from Dare.

Eddie felt as if he'd really accomplished something then.

And it set the tone for the rest of the tour. Dare relaxed, and while he seemed a little socially awkward, he was generally charming and always intelligent.

The beer was damned good too, even the flavored one that had a spicy kick to it. When they'd completed the tour and gotten their souvenir mugs, Dare seemed reluctant to show them out. Dee had left at some point or was in another part of the building. Eddie hadn't seen her since they'd first come in. Eddie was finishing up with his order for another taxi when Dare spoke again.

"Y'all should come back for one of the regular tours on the weekends, when we have a live band playing and game going on. It gets crazy fun."

Dare came off almost bashful when he said it.

Eddie patted Carter's arm. "Well, I'm a park ranger over at Big Bend, and I won't have weekends off for a while. Carter usually spends the weekends with me there, but he could stay in Odessa and—"

"I'll wait for you," Carter said smoothly. "But, Dare, if you're interested, we'd love to have you over for dinner some evening. Eddie's here a couple of nights a week. If you want, I'll give you our phone numbers and we can set a date for it."

Dare was definitely blushing and Eddie was quite aware of his attempt to covertly shield his groin with his hands.

"Um." Dare sputtered for a few seconds then exhaled loudly. "God, I'm such a nerd. I—" He looked at Carter first before staring Eddie in the eyes. "What would it be? Are you…are you two talking about as friends? Because maybe I'm reading everything wrong and being a presumptuous idiot, but I thought… I mean, were you — ?"

Eddie decided to rescue him from his babbling. "We were meaning it as a date with the both of us, and yeah, we were checking you out. We like what we've seen of you so far."

Dare's eyes bugged and his mouth dropped open.

"I hope that's not a no," Carter said. "If it is, that's okay. If it isn't, you need to know that Eddie and I aren't into casual sex. We're looking for a man who'd be faithful to us and we'd be the same."

"But you two are already together," Dare pointed out. "There's a bond there someone new wouldn't be a part of."

Eddie took a chance and gently cupped one of Dare's hands in between both of his. "Our bond, as you call it, had to start somewhere. We began our relationship on honesty, both of us knowing what the other needed to feel complete and happy. Any man we bring in will grow to be just as important to us as we are to each other." Eddie hoped. He still wondered if he'd ever feel as strongly for anyone else as he did for Carter. He'd sure try, for the right partner, whether that turned out to be Dare or not.

"No pressure."

At hearing Carter's words, Eddie released Dare's hand. "What he said. Carter and I are aware of how unusual what we're proposing is."

Dare finally managed to close his mouth, only to open it again. "Just a date? I mean, just a meal and conversation?"

Dare sure was nervous. He must have been intrigued, too, because he hadn't bolted or told them to fuck off.

"Think about it, or not." Carter took a business card off the desk and picked up a pen, too. "I'll leave our numbers."

Dare cleared his throat. "If, ah... If I decided to do this, do I call or text one of you? Both?" He frowned. "Is one of you going to get mad that he isn't the first? I could do a group message—"

Dare was considering it. Eddie wanted to let out a whoop but figured that would totally not be appropriate.

Carter jotted down their numbers then handed the card to Dare, speaking as he did so. "Neither of us are like that, Dare. This is something we want. It's not a game. Eddie and I will understand if it's too weird for you, and neither of us is going to flip out if you contact the other."

Dare licked his lips. "What if I'm not as attracted to one of you as I am to the other, or the reverse? Say Carter is into me but Eddie, you're just going along with it?"

"Which is why we'd like to get to know you, and for you to get to know us," Eddie explained. "So again, no pressure. If you're interested, that's great. If not, we'll still be buying your beer."

"Think about it if you want to," Carter added. "It is just a meal and conversation, but if it goes further than that, we'd need to all talk about what we wanted, needed, and expected. Thanks for the tour."

"You're welcome," Dare replied, tucking the card into his shirt pocket. "And about the offer, I'm flattered. I don't know why you'd ask me, but I'll... I'll consider it and get back with y'all. It might be a week or so. I really am swamped trying to run this business."

"But you love it." Eddie understood that and thought it was a good sign of Dare's ability to commit. "Later. And thanks."

He and Carter left. Eddie wasn't sure about Dare being the right man for them, but he was aware of the potential there.

"Was that okay?" Carter asked once they were a decent distance from the building.

Eddie had to think for a few seconds before he realized what Carter was referring to. "That you asked him out? Sure. I was right there with you. He's an interesting guy."

"Shy, too, if I'm not mistaken. The tours must be a challenge for him," Carter said. "It's odd. Shy usually isn't a quality that I'm attracted to. I like confidence." He looked Eddie over appreciatively. "Someone who takes control."

"But you like fucking Georgie, too, and he's—well, he's kind of bossy, isn't he?" Eddie rethought his words. *That was an understatement.*

"He's very vocal about what he wants," Carter said with more diplomacy than Eddie would ever have.

"Not shy at all," Eddie agreed.

Carter nodded, and waved at the cab just as he had earlier. It made Eddie stupidly happy to see him do it and know that he was learning more of Carter's quirks.

"Anyway, so it's strange to find myself attracted to someone so different from that," Carter continued.

Eddie thought he might have an answer for it. "You have the confidence and strength in me. Maybe you're ready for someone different to complement those qualities."

The way Carter looked at him had Eddie convinced he could move mountains for the man. He would sure try, because Carter meant so much to him and Eddie wasn't going to be able to keep from admitting his love for Carter for much longer.

Chapter Seven

Carter was trying really hard not to squawk like a chicken and flee.

"It's going to be fine. You'll love it," Eddie said, holding open the door to the tattoo and piercing shop. "We can leave, if you want," he added when Carter's legs wouldn't listen to his brain and move.

"No. I want this," Carter found the balls to say. He did, but his tits already ached with imagined pain. Which, in turn, made his dick hard. He ghosted one hand over it. "Obviously."

"We can come back, if you're too scared."

It was the exactly right thing to say to goad him on. Carter didn't think that was what Eddie meant to do, but it worked to propel him through the door. A girl with purple hair and more facial piercings than Carter could count without appearing to be rude greeted them.

"Hey. Welcome to Tats and Tips. You have an appointment?"

Carter wanted to know how she kept the gum she was smacking on from sticking to any of the piece of metal in her lips, tongue and—this one made him cringe, likely outside just as he did inside—that little strip of skin between her top lip and her gum. At least he thought that was where the hoop beneath her lip was shoved through.

"We do. Carter is supposed to see Mike R." Eddie stepped up to the counter. "Do I pay now?"

"If you do and he backs out, no refunds." She eyed Carter with what he suspected was a little bit of disdain. "Might be better to wait."

"Pay her," he snapped, bristling at the insult to his pride. He'd been intending to argue with Eddie over who was paying for it all, but fuck it. Eddie could have the privilege.

Eddie pulled out his wallet. "I'd have paid for the piercings even if you hadn't just poked at him. Carter won't back out once he's given his word."

"Whatever. He has a penis, ergo he's a liar."

Eddie scowled at her. "Wow, I'm guessing that level of misandry wouldn't be tolerated by the owner."

"Rain, are you being a shit again?" asked a tall, bulky man with even more facial piercings than the woman. "Sorry if she is," he said to Eddie and Carter. "I'm Mike. She's my sister and half owner here. I'd fire her if I could."

"Whatever. That's what happens when you make me work the front, asshole." Rain took Eddie's credit card. "Then you expect me to be *nice* to guys after Brian cheated on me with that—"

"Rain, shut up," Mike snapped. "Jesus. Take some of your nerve pills or go have a toke."

"I'll lock the front door then." Rain processed his payment then handed it back to him, along with the receipt and some other papers. "Sign these. I'm due some misandry, if that means snarking at men. You have any idea how many assholes have something to say about these?" She touched one of her breasts.

"We don't," Carter informed her. "Blaming us for your man trouble is like me blaming you because some woman was rude to me. Fortunately, I'm more level-headed than that and will just blame you for being obnoxious."

Rain glared. "You haven't looked at my boobs."

Carter glared back. "Why would I?"

"Children," Eddie rumbled.

Carter turned his glare to Eddie. "Really?"

Eddie blanched. "Okay, okay, calm down. She's wrong. You're right. She's being childish. You aren't. Can you sign the consent form?"

"Good," Carter huffed. "And yes." He did so with a flair that would have made any drama mama proud.

"Oh, I get it. You two are..." Rain pointed one finger and made a circle with her finger and thumb on the other hand.

"Rain! Out!" Mike yelled.

Rain smirked but came out from behind the counter. "Prude."

Carter assumed she was referring to her brother, who should have had steam coming out from his ears, since he appeared to be exceedingly angry.

"Sorry again. She's moody," Mike stated. "Please, come back to the piercing room."

Carter's irritation morphed into apprehension. He wouldn't have let it show for anything. Holding his head high, Carter followed Mike. Eddie was right behind them both.

"So you wanted both nips done, right?" Mike asked when he stopped at a sink.

"Yes, please," Carter answered. Surely he was a dumbass for asking a man to please shove a needle through his nipples.

"You'll love them if you have sensitive tits — or even if you don't. Some people swear having them pierced increases sensitivity or creates it if there was none before." Mike washed his hands, and Carter was glad to see that he scrubbed them quite thoroughly.

"Have a seat right there on the table."

The table was padded, much like a massage table as far as Carter could tell. He sat and Eddie stood beside him.

"You'll need to take your shirt off," Mike continued while he put on gloves.

Carter quit watching him. The shop was clean, well-maintained, and he'd seen the autoclaved packages laid out on the metal tray. That was all he needed to know, besides the fact that Mike was supposed to be the best in Odessa at what he did.

Which is sticking needles into people's body parts.

"Looking a little pale," Eddie murmured. "We can —"

Carter growled and pulled his shirt off over his head. He handed it to Eddie. "I think you'd look good with yours done too."

To his surprise, Eddie started taking off his shirt. Carter gawped at him.

"I was going to wait until yours were done to let you know I'm next." Eddie sighed and rolled his eyes. "But no. You ruined it."

Mike clucked his tongue. "Guys, guys, it's all good. At least I'm not the one who spilled the beans, thank God. I suck at keeping secrets and was afraid I'd blow it."

Carter was still trying to wrap his mind around the fact that Eddie was getting pierced too. "You don't care for—" He stopped before he could utterly humiliate himself.

"TMI, guys. I don't want to hear about anyone's sex life when I don't have one." Mike held up a small wipe. "I'm going to clean the right one off first, then mark it. Left is after, and once you're happy with the marks, I'll pierce you."

Carter's nipple stood erect after being cleaned with alcohol. He forced himself to take deep, steady breaths.

"Doing good, man." Mike pinched at the first nipple. "Don't get territorial or nothing. Just gotta make it bigger for the clamp."

"Clamp? What clamp?" Carter could be excused for the way his voice broke.

Mike held one up. "This one. It goes on your nipple and makes it a lot easier to get the needle through quickly. Believe me when I tell you this clamp is your friend."

Carter wasn't sure about that but he didn't argue. He sat very still while Mark prepared him.

"They look good?" Mike asked, handing Carter a mirror before glancing at Eddie. "What do you think?"

Carter saw that the dots where the needle would enter were perfectly matched on each tit. "Good. Whenever you're ready."

"Same. You're gonna look gorgeous, honey," Eddie told Carter.

Carter would get a lot more piercings if it meant Eddie being mushy like that. "Okay. Do it."

He thought he'd shake apart, but when the needle was shoved through, Carter didn't cry out. To his embarrassment, he moaned like a porn star.

"That's hot, huh," Mike said. "I've had some people actually orgasm when the needle goes through."

"Oh God," Carter panted. He was afraid he just might be one of those people when Mike did the other one.

Eddie's lusty expression didn't help. Carter was so close to the edge he could taste the ecstasy.

Then Mike slid the bar through. Carter clamped down every muscle in his body to keep from coming.

"Nice," Eddie crooned.

"No messing with them for two weeks," Mike warned. "Well, if you're gentle and your hands are clean, but no mouth to tit action. That could lead to an infection."

The second piercing felt even better. Carter maintained his dignity, mostly, only moaning a little. He didn't come in his pants, so he counted it a victory.

Then Eddie took his place and Carter's dick was harder than it'd ever been in his life as Mike pierced Eddie's right nipple.

Eddie closed his eyes, his lips parting on a soft exhalation. "Oh man, that's weird."

"Good weird?" Carter asked.

Mike slid the barbell in.

"Ah," Mike panted.

"Good weird," Carter decided, knowing Eddie's expressions well. He was turned on just like Carter had been. That and the hard-on were dead giveaways.

"Y'all should consider a guiche or a Prince Albert," Mike said.

Carter's dick tried to wither away. "No to that dick one. What's the other?"

Mike laughed. "The PA ain't so bad. I have one and love it, but it does put you out of commission for a while. The guiche is a piercing right behind your balls on your perineum. It's great to tug and suck on."

"We'll think about it." Carter *was* thinking about it, damn it. He'd do some research before he got one. *If I get one. Oh who am I kidding? I'll probably do it.*

Mike didn't make a sound when his left nipple was pierced. He still had that erection, and Carter wanted to get him home immediately.

"Here's the aftercare instructions. If there's any problems or questions, call me. That's my cell number on the bottom there." Mike handed the paper to Carter, since Eddie was easing his shirt back on. "See you soon for that guiche."

Eddie raked Carter with a look that made his blood heat with arousal.

"I'll call for the cab."

Carter chatted with Mike while Eddie made the call. All the while, Carter was extremely aware of his throbbing nipples. Every move he made, even if it was just to breathe, set off numerous bolts of pleasure that spiraled from his chest to every part of his body. If he kept that up, he wasn't going to make it home without losing it.

After Mike let them out, Carter didn't talk much and neither did Eddie. The sexual tension between them grew by the minute. Carter waved at the taxi driver when the cab turned the corner by them. For some reason that seemed to amuse Eddie.

Unfortunately for them, they landed a talkative cabbie. Carter tried to make noises during the man's pauses but didn't care if he succeeded in his attempts. All he could do was think about how much he wanted Eddie.

Carter was vaguely aware of that odd being-watched sensation after he and Eddie got out by the apartment. He didn't mention it. Nothing was going to happen to him and Eddie, and despite their earlier talk about the matter, Carter was flying too high on endorphins and lust to worry.

They went inside and Eddie locked the door. He pointed to the bedroom.

Carter spun around and marched—or tried to. Eddie swatted his backside once, then again and it jostled Carter all over—especially his nipples. It was like a livewire of bliss had suddenly sprouted between them and his ass.

Eddie growled and Carter was pushed chest-first against the wall. He slapped his hands to it, bracing himself just as Eddie started spanking him. The swats were harder than usual, probably because Carter was naked when Eddie really started in on his backside.

But he wasn't now, and he moaned with every slap to his butt. Carter arched his back, needing more. What he got was Eddie pressed to him and biting at his shoulder.

Carter yelped and shoved a hand down to grab his cock. He needed to come. That was all there was to it.

Eddie batted his hand aside. He unfastened Carter's jeans then fisted his dick.

"Yes," Carter hissed, tossing his head back. "Fuck, make me come."

All it took was a stroke over his crown and the feel of Eddie's teeth at his shoulder, and Carter shouted as he lost it, cum jetting onto the wall.

Eddie pumped him until he was dry, sucked at the bite mark until Carter was ready to beg to be fucked.

Then Eddie stepped back and slapped Carter's ass again. He took Carter by the hand and led him to the bedroom. There Eddie kissed him, a slow, devouring kiss that Carter sank into completely.

Eddie ran his hands over Carter's back and butt, and lightly rubbed his chest over Carter's.

Carter couldn't handle so much pleasure. He started to pull back.

Eddie did so first, only to grab Carter's T-shirt at the neck before ripping it apart. "Always wanted to do that," he muttered, gaze on Carter's chest. "Goddamn, those are so pretty. I wish I could —" Eddie dipped his head down and nuzzled over one tit, keeping clear of Carter's nipple.

Carter wove his fingers through Eddie's hair. "Wish you could too. God, do I wish you could."

"Soon." Eddie licked a path down to Carter's stomach. At the same time, he pushed Carter's pants and briefs down. He knelt and turned his dark gaze upward. "I want to do everything to you. You have no idea how much I think about you." He bent then and tongued Carter's belly button.

Carter had the impression Eddie had been on the verge of saying more, but he didn't push. God knew he was holding back his own confession, and maybe that was the best considering they'd met a potential boyfriend for them. A potential partner.

Eddie lapped at Carter's soft cock until it began to firm up again. He palmed Carter's balls, then pinched the skin behind them.

"Ungh!" Carter couldn't do anything but loose raw sounds as Eddie kept it up, licking and sucking on his tip, pinching and rubbing the spot behind his nuts. Before long Carter was thrusting his hips, wanting more of Eddie's mouth, more of the pain he brought that mixed so well with the pleasure.

Eddie gave it to him, cupping Carter's balls in one hand and squeezing his left thigh with bruising strength with the other.

Carter grabbed onto Eddie's shoulders and stared blearily at his cock sinking deeper into Eddie's mouth.

Inside, his organs jittered and shook as his body geared up for another mind-melting release.

Eddie applied pressure to Carter's balls, enough to keep him from getting too close to coming. He took Carter's dick in to the root, his tongue soft and wet as he flicked it all the way down Carter's length.

Then he swallowed, and the constriction of those throat muscles around Carter's cockhead was as close to a spiritual experience as Carter had ever gotten.

Eddie rumbled, probably laughing and proud of himself, as he came back up. "On the bed. Ass up for me so I can beat your sweet butt."

"The paddle," Carter requested. He needed something harder than Eddie's hand. "Or..." The visual he got made him shiver. "Your belt." It would sting and burn and he suddenly wanted that fiercely.

"Are you sure?" Eddie asked, toying with his belt buckle. "We haven't used it before. You might hate it."

"If I do, you'll stop. We'll use the safe words we discussed a few weeks ago. Red, stop, yellow, pause, green, go. Okay? You know I'll use them if I need to."

Eddie nodded. "Yeah you will. Get on the bed."

Carter scrambled onto his knees then bent and lowered his chest to the bed. He hissed, having for the moment forgotten about his nipples. "God, I'm gonna be hard at work all day tomorrow because of these things!"

"Good." Eddie caressed his ass then spread his cheeks.

It was always hard for Carter not to pull away when Eddie did that, exposed his hole so fully. That was probably why Eddie did it, pushing Carter like Carter craved for him to do.

He loved a little bit of humiliation, much to his shock.

"Look at this." Eddie thumped his pucker and Carter almost rattled out of his skin.

"I can't see it," he ground out.

Eddie rubbed over the spot he'd tapped. "Could take a pic for you. I'll hand my phone to you right after."

Carter had been about to say no when it occurred to him that he trusted Eddie completely. "Do it," he urged.

Eddie's harsh exhalation told of his arousal. "Gladly. You're fucking amazing, honey."

"I know," Carter joked, adjusting his legs until his knees were further apart.

"Good. You oughta know." Eddie patted his butt then startled Carter by smacking him right in the center of it.

"Eddie!" Carter closed his eyes and struggled for control. He wanted to jack off so bad.

Eddie pushed one cheek aside. "Nice, baby."

Carter heard the clicking of the camera as Eddie took pictures. "Want my thumb? You need it dry and shoved into you?"

Mewling counted as an answer. Carter knew it did because it got him what he wanted.

When Eddie pushed the tip of his thumb into Carter's ass, the dry burn sent an amazing tendril of ecstasy up to his dick.

"Open your eyes," Eddie said. He slid his thumb out.

Carter's protest died on his lips when he opened his eyes at the same time the phone landed by his head.

"Video and pics," Eddie told him. "Watch it while I do this."

"Do—" Carter was reaching for the phone when he heard the belt slicing through the air. He tensed and shot forward when it hit his ass. "Oh!"

"Too much?" Eddie asked, a worried note to his voice.

"No, no. Green. Bright, bright green." Carter clutched the phone. He must have at some point pressed play because as Eddie spanked him, he watched a clip of Eddie playing with his asshole.

Carter shoved back into every stinging blow. His buttocks felt like they were on flaming and if he flopped over onto his back, he halfway expected that the sheets would catch fire.

Eddie worked him over good, keeping the spanks from being too hard or too light. When he stopped, Carter's eyelids were almost too heavy to keep open and he had no idea what he'd done with the phone. He didn't care, either.

"I gotta fuck you," Eddie said in a guttural tone. "Now."

Carter would have let him just ram right in, but some part of him picked up on the ripping of the condom wrapper and the gurgling of the lube.

Thankfully Eddie didn't waste any more time than that. He pushed his fat cock into Carter, spreading him open with it. They'd fucked often enough that Carter could take it without being loosened up first.

Eddie still went slowly, moving into Carter in short thrusts that seemed to take forever to complete.

Then Carter was so full of dick he could have died happy. Eddie's balls slapped against his, and Eddie held him by one shoulder and one hip.

"Down," Eddie growled, moving the hand from Carter's shoulder to his nape. The weight he put there turned Carter's crank even further.

"You like me holding you down, fucking you like this," Eddie got out between grunts while he ground his groin against Carter's ass. "I could walk in, throw you down on the floor, rip your pants off then fuck you dry and raw, and you'd let me, wouldn't you?"

Not only would Carter let him, Carter wanted Eddie to use him in such a way.

He didn't say as much because Eddie pulled almost fully out then thrust back in. From there on it was a hard fast fuck, all base needs and animalistic sounds coming from them. Carter had never felt so much a man before, nor so close to a primitive being at the same time.

Eddie rammed into him repeatedly, then surprised Carter by pulling out fully. He flipped Carter over onto his back.

Carter gasped, his backside flaring with heat again. Eddie parted Carter's legs, hooked Carter's ankles over Eddie's shoulders then thrust back in.

Carter keened and flailed, everything was too much. The pleasure, the love threatening to burst out of him. He shoved a fist to his mouth and used his other hand to reach for his dick.

Eddie hunkered down, hips flying when he sealed his mouth over Carter's.

Carter jerked off with sloppy, harsh strokes that would leave him raw. He tried to rock his butt up but his leverage was skewed and it didn't matter because he was coming, his vision blurring, breath sputtering.

"Fuck," Eddie drove in deep. "Fuck yeah," he got out. "Carter." He pushed in a little more. "Honey, I—" Eddie moaned, hips stuttering in a rapid-fire assault against Carter's ass.

If he was lucky, he'd have bruises from where Eddie's hip bones battered his butt.

Eddie huffed and panted. He shook as he came.

Carter held onto him, smearing his own spunk onto Eddie's skin.

Later, the guilt hit him as Eddie slept beside him. What they had together was fantastic. Why wasn't he able to say Eddie was everything he wanted, when Eddie clearly was?

Because I'm a greedy, selfish bastard, that's why.

But the guilt was met by the memory of Eddie's appreciation for Dare hours earlier, and those two things chased Carter into sleep.

Chapter Eight

"Mom, now's not a good time," Eddie repeated. He'd spent hours out with three other park rangers trying to find the bobcat that had attacked a child that morning. There were signs warning hikers that small children were at risk from such attacks. It didn't stop people, and it had almost cost a six-year-old girl her life.

Combine the attack with the fact that her parents hadn't been properly prepared for a hike — they'd only taken a bottle of water each, a pack of energy bars, and their cell phones, for God's sake — and it was a miracle the child hadn't died. Cell service was spotty at best and non-existent in a great deal of the park. The parents had to carry the child for over two miles before someone had heard their cries for help.

Eddie had gone back to headquarters, along with the other rangers he'd been searching with, because they'd found nothing so far. Not even tracks. The hikers had either lied about where they'd been or they'd gotten confused. Eddie was inclined to think it was the latter. They'd been panicked as hell when he'd spoken with them.

"I want to meet this man who has made you forget your family," his mother said sharply. "No phone calls for weeks, just a little text to this brother or that sister. One to your dad."

"Well, if you had a cell phone—"

"Edward Allan Canales, I will come to Big Bend and thump some sense into you! Or better yet, Odessa—"

"Mom, no," Eddie whined, knowing she could—and would—drive from Albuquerque to Odessa. She'd find Carter somehow, too. His mom was more than a force of Nature. She was…scary.

"It's not even a six hour drive to Odessa," she continued. "Not the way I drive."

"Mom, I'm sorry, okay? I've just…I really like him." Eddie touched one nipple through his shirt. "I more than like him, and I'm sorry I've been so wrapped up in Carter that I haven't called you."

"Carter, hm? And were you dating this man the last time we talked?"

Eddie had been, and he'd been exceedingly careful not to mention Carter's name. *Too bad I fucked up and said it now.* "Yes, Mom, I was, but I wasn't sure how it would work out." Not if his mom butted in, anyway. He was afraid she'd be too much for Carter.

"You've had plenty of time to tell me since, Eddie. You hurt my feelings and I don't appreciate it."

"I'm sorry," he said again. "I love you. You know that. I won't wait weeks to call you again."

The promise didn't placate her. "I don't care. I want to meet this Carter. What's his last name?"

Eddie's older brother Tino was a cop. There was no chance in hell he would give his mom—and through her, Tino—Carter's name so they could snoop around.

Eddie settled for distraction. "I love him, Mom, okay? I haven't told him yet, because I want the time to be just right. I've been spending all my spare time with Carter, and because of that, I know what I feel is true and enduring. So maybe you can not be so mad at me, and please don't blame Carter." He tacked on the piece de resistance. "Why don't you and Pop come out at the end of August, when I can take a few days off? Then you can see me and meet Carter, too."

"I know what you're doing," she said. "I'll think about it, or I might turn up there."

Eddie didn't ask which there she meant. "I have to go, Mom. We had a bobcat maul a child today."

"And have you found it? Is the child okay?"

"She's going to live, but she'll have scars, and no, ma'am—"

"Why are you talking to me then? Go find this animal!"

Eddie just kept from sighing. "I will. Love you. I'll call on my next day off."

"Love you too, son. If you don't call—"

"I will. Gotta go." He disconnected the call. Eddie tucked the phone into his pocket and went back into the building.

"I was just coming to get you," said Israel, a fellow park ranger. "Everyone's finished eating and are ready to start discussing what our next steps should be."

"Okay. Let me just send a text." He took his phone out again so he could let Carter know he'd likely be unavailable for hours—possibly even overnight, if they ended up camping out in their hunt for the cat.

Carter texted back in seconds with an *Okay, be careful.* Eddie put his phone away again. He had a job to do.

* * * *

Eddie straggled into his RV the following evening, worn out and hungry. It said something that he chose to shower first. His cell phone had been dead, so dead he couldn't turn it on at first, but once he'd scrubbed the grunge off and gotten clean, he checked the phone. It booted up and he saw that he had several texts and two missed calls. One from Carter, the other an unknown number.

Eddie called Carter back first, ignoring the voicemails.

"Hey, I'm glad you called," Carter said.

"I'm glad, too. I was going to come out tonight, but I'm beat." He really hated to miss out on a night with Carter, but driving when he could barely keep his eyes open was stupid.

"Stay there. I was thinking of taking a couple of days off. Would it be okay if I spent them with you?"

"That would be perfect," Eddie said, his exhaustion lessening at the thought of Carter being there.

"Oh good. I'll be there in a few hours then, but you sleep."

"A few hours?" Eddie wasn't going to be able to sleep knowing Carter would be there. "You already took off?"

Carter was silent for a moment and it unnerved Eddie. "Carter? What's wrong?"

"Nothing's wrong, per se, and I haven't taken off just yet. I wanted to call you first and not just show up. There's...damn it..." He mumbled something Eddie couldn't make out.

"What was that?" Eddie asked.

"You were right," Carter repeated. "I asked about Mark. He quit his job while he was in California. Becca doesn't know where he is, and she won't tell me why he might have quit. It would be unprofessional, but I think something happened."

"And you still feel like you're being watched?"

"Almost daily," Carter confirmed. "I'm jumping at shadows. Thought a few days away would help."

"Of course. I hope you told Becca about Mark, that he'd been harassing you before he left."

Carter's answer didn't surprise Eddie.

"No, I didn't. There was no reason to, and she probably would have lectured me for not coming to her sooner. The thing was, he didn't do anything I could prove."

"Consider telling her anyway, please. It might get you some information, and I can ask my brother Tino to see if he can dig anything up on Mark."

"Tino's the cop?" Carter asked.

"Yeah, and he's a bossy pain in the ass, but he'll try to help us." Eddie sat on the bed. "Are you packed?"

"Yeah. I was thinking about driving out, even if I didn't hear from you soon. I miss you."

"I miss you too," Eddie confessed. "Why don't you get your bag and backpack, and load up while we're talking?"

"You're worried about me going outside here?" Carter asked.

"I also just want to talk to you, honey. It's the best thing I've got to do in days."

Eddie listened to Carter talk about his work and answered questions about the fruitless hunt for the bobcat. When Carter was in the Jeep and ready to drive, Eddie got off the phone with him

Wired instead of worn out now, Eddie listened to his voicemails. The first was from Carter, a sweet message about missing him, but the second one surprised Eddie.

"Er, hi. Hi Eddie, I mean, this is Dare. Dare Habrock. I'm calling about dinner with you and, um, Carter? If y'all are still interested, I am. I mean, I'd like to do it. Uh. That. Dinner! I'd like to have dinner with y'all sometime. And, I hope it's okay I called you first. So, maybe you could let me know, huh? Thanks."

It was a test, Eddie suspected. Not a mean-spirited one, just a way for Dare to see if it really was okay for him to call one of them.

Eddie wanted to call Carter, but wouldn't while he was driving. He did send a text letting Carter know he was about to set up a dinner date for the three of them. He trusted Carter not to mess with his phone until he made a stop for gas, food, or the toilet—if he did stop at all.

Then Eddie took a deep breath and dialed Dare back, since he'd left the message for Eddie the night before.

"Hello?" Dare sounded uncertain, or nervous.

Eddie wished he could see Dare's face. "Hey, I'm sorry I missed your call. We had a bobcat attack at the national park yesterday and several of us park rangers spent the night out in the middle of nowhere trying to find the cat. Unsuccessfully, I might add."

"Oh. Oh, okay. I was worried—never mind."

Eddie smiled even though Dare couldn't see him. "Honesty's always good, man. Tell me what you thought."

Dare coughed or cleared his throat. Eddie couldn't tell for certain.

"I, er, I thought maybe you and Carter had changed your mind. Minds. God, this is confusing."

Eddie laughed softly, delighted by Dare. "It is, but we're all smart. We can figure out the details." He decided not to bring up that Dare hadn't tried to call Carter when he'd not heard from Eddie quickly.

"I was afraid to try a second time," Dare said. "I thought... Well, I thought if you didn't call back, y'all had decided I wouldn't do, or else Carter got mad because I called you and not him. That sounds stupid, but this is all... Eddie, I haven't even dated a man in years. Years. With the cancer then starting the business, and there's other reasons."

"Are you wanting me to ask what those reasons are?" Eddie couldn't tell.

"No, I'm not playing a game like that. It's just that there *are* reasons I'm not ready to share. I don't see the point in doing so if this goes nowhere."

"Gotcha. I'll respect that and so will Carter. Now." Eddie dropped his voice a little lower into what he hoped was a sexy drawl. "When were you interested in getting together for dinner?"

Three hours after Eddie got off the phone with Dare, he was dozing on the couch when Carter arrived. Carter had a key to the RV since it was Eddie's home. Eddie watched in that sleep-wake stupor as the door was opened. Carter came in, and everything in Eddie's world was right.

"I love you, you know," he said, more alert than he sounded.

Carter dropped his backpack and his duffle bag. "You're not even awake."

"I'm awake enough to know what I said and to mean it." Eddie got up and opened his arms.

Carter all but ran to him, crossing the distance in a few long strides.

Eddie embraced him and buried his nose in Carter's soft hair. "I mean it, so much. I love you." And his heart was unlimited. Eddie knew that now. He could love Carter and another man as long as he wanted to do so. He didn't have to limit himself to societal expectations and norms. Carter had always seen that. The man was smart, and also staring at Eddie with adoration.

"I love you too, Eddie. I—" Carter glanced away.

Eddie cupped his chin and pulled his head back around. "Out with it before I kiss you senseless."

Carter batted his lashes, putting on a coy look Eddie had never seen him do before. "Kiss me now, then we can talk."

If it was a deflection, Eddie would go with it for now. He slanted his mouth over Carter's and slid his tongue between Carter's parted lips. Carter wrapped his arms around Eddie and they held each other while enjoying the kiss.

More than enjoying—Eddie wanted to lay Carter out and lick every inch of him. Almost every inch. They still had a week to go before their nipples were cleared for mouths.

But Eddie didn't lay Carter down. Instead he took Carter by the hand and had him sit on the couch. Eddie was right beside him. "Now what was it you were going to say?"

Carter sighed heavily and folded his hands together on his lap. He stared down then looked at Eddie. "I just wonder if I shouldn't just toss the idea of having another man with us. I always wanted that kind of relationship, maybe because of some insecurity or something, I don't know. It's just always been my idea of perfection for me. But that was before I fell in love with you."

Eddie tipped his head to one side. "Did you check your phone?"

"I did." Carter unfolded his hands. He took his phone out of his pocket. "I was happy. Now I wonder if I'm not just a selfish prick."

"I don't think you are." Eddie pulled Carter onto his lap, encouraging Carter to straddle his legs. Once Carter was settled, Eddie dipped his head and kissed Carter's chest, right above his heart. "What I believe is, you have a big heart with a great capacity for love. There's nothing wrong with sharing that love. And you know what else?"

Carter scooted closer until his rigid cock was pressed against Eddie's stomach. "What?"

Eddie's thoughts scrambled but he pulled them back together. "I think Dare needs us. If it works out, we won't love each other any less. We'll have more love between the three of us."

"You really believe that?" Carter asked.

"I do." Eddie kissed Carter again while cupping Carter's ass. He gave those firm globes a good squeeze.

Carter thrust against his belly.

Eddie twined his tongue with Carter's, taking control of the kiss in a more demanding way. He pushed his hands down the back of Carter's pants, needing skin.

Carter moaned and rutted faster. Sounds slipped from him into Eddie, fueling Eddie's desire.

He twisted around and pinned Carter down on the couch. It meant breaking the kiss. It also meant he could get Carter's pants undone. When he had Carter's dick in hand, Eddie couldn't hold back a confession. "I want to ditch the condoms when you're ready. I've been tested since the hookup with Georgie, and I'll do it again."

"I've never—" Carter gulped. "I want to. I was tested right before then. I'll go to the clinic when I get back to Odessa."

Eddie's response was a wet suck on Carter's cockhead.

Carter cursed and bowed his back, pushing his shaft deeper into Eddie's mouth.

Eddie pressed down on Carter's hips, holding him as still as he could. He took Carter in to the base of his cock and inhaled through his nose when he had it in Carter's pubes. He smelled soap and sweat, the heady odor of his lover. Eddie couldn't get enough of the scent.

He swallowed and delighted in Carter's garbled shout. *He'd* done that to his beautiful, strong man, had pushed him to the point of incoherency in seconds. Eddie came up and suckled the fat tip, working his tongue in the slit. The spongy head was possibly his favorite part of Carter's dick. Eddie increased the suction on it while at the same time tracing over Carter's hole.

"Please," Carter got out after several attempts. Nothing else had been an actual word.

Eddie had to lick his way down Carter's erection. He took his time at it, then with a little maneuvering he sucked Carter's entire nut sac into his mouth.

"Eddie!" Carter grabbed at his hair.

Eddie hummed and pulled back a little. He let Carter's balls go with a wet *pop* and nosed over his perineum. He needed better access to Carter's pucker and wasn't going to get it on the couch. Eddie shoved the coffee table aside with one hand. It was a cheap one he'd planned on chucking for a nicer one eventually, so he didn't care if it broke.

What he cared about was getting Carter naked. "Off," he snarled, pushing Carter's shirt up.

Carter took it from there, whipping the Henley off.

"I can't wait to suck these," Eddie said. He brushed his fingers over Carter's nipples.

"Aw, shit. I can't wait for that, either." Carter began trying to get his pants off. "Fucking shoes!"

Eddie pressed down on Carter's nipples, watching his face for signs that it was too painful. When Carter tried pushing his chest up into the touches, Eddie knew it was all good. He flicked each nipple ring then moved to help Carter get his shoes and socks off. After those, it was easy to tug down his pants and underwear. Eddie tossed them aside and removed his shorts, the only clothing he had on.

Then he was free to touch and taste Carter. Eddie positioned Carter with his chest on the couch and his knees on the floor.

"Can you take pictures again?" Carter asked.

"Gonna be busy." Eddie licked down Carter's crease then raised his head. "We could set up one of our phones to record next time when I won't have my hands free."

"Anything," Carter said breathlessly. "Whatever you want, just don't stop doing that."

Eddie spread Carter's cheeks wide. "This?" he asked, then repeated the wet stroke from a moment ago.

"Uh huh. That." Carter wiggled his butt. "Eat me, Eddie."

Since there wasn't a please on that, Eddie figured Carter wanted a little pain to take him out of his mind, help him get away from his worries. Carter wasn't the one to give out the orders, even if he did control everything with just one of three words.

"You get my hand." He wasn't getting up to find a belt. Eddie first kissed Carter's pucker, then he sat back and started laying swats all over Carter's backside. The bruises from the belt had faded, and Eddie wasn't spanking hard enough to leave new ones. He didn't think Carter wanted hard. He just wanted an escape.

Eddie gave it to him, spanking his ass and talking dirty. "When we get our tests back, and they're clean, I'm gonna fuck you and come in you. I'm not pulling out when I'm done. I'll keep my dick buried there until I can go again, then I'll soak your ass with my seed." He was glad Carter couldn't see his expression. 'Seed' felt wrong on Eddie's tongue, but he hadn't been able to think of a better word. "I'm gonna mark you inside. After I come the second time, I might stay in for a third time. Your hole will be red and swollen, hot where it grips my dick. Or," Eddie pulled one cheek aside. He tapped Carter's pucker with one knuckle.

"I might just take my dick out and put my mouth right here." He tapped again. "Might lick you clean and come up to share my cum with you again, push it into your mouth with my tongue."

"Fuck," Carter rasped. "Eddie, harder."

Eddie let the next blow carry more force. He wasn't really sure he'd do the snowballing-pass-the-cum-from-Carter's-ass thing ever, but it was hot to talk about it.

Another couple of swats and Eddie pressed Carter's cheeks apart then went after his hole. He pushed his tongue right in, rubbed the outside of it with his thumbs.

Carter bucked and pushed back, trying to fuck himself on Eddie's tongue. Eddie used his arm strength to shove Carter forward. He growled and nipped the tender skin above Carter's hole. "Who's leading here?" he demanded.

"You," Carter replied. "You are."

"Remember that." Eddie nibbled his way over Carter's ring. He licked until it was soaked, then slid two fingers in alongside his tongue.

Eddie curled his fingers after a few thrusts and found Carter's gland. He loved the sounds Carter made when his prostate was touched just so. Mindless, wanton sounds that fired Eddie's lust even more.

Eddie fingered Carter roughly, with bold strokes that had his knuckles rubbing over the outer rim. He had to quit tonguing Carter but that was okay. He felt Carter inside, the soft inner walls of his ass, the way they clenched and rippled around his fingers.

He took the lube out from under the couch where he'd stashed it while waiting for Carter. Eddie took the cap off with his teeth. He poured some of the viscous stuff right onto Carter's hole and began pushing it into him.

The lube made it easy to slide a third finger, then a fourth, into Carter. Eddie was careful not to do damage. He soaked Carter's hole in wetness and gentled his thrusts.

"Someday I will put my whole hand in you." Eddie teased at that now, flicking his thumb over the outside of Carter's stretched pucker. He kept his other four digits buried in Carter's body. "My whole hand. We'll film that for sure, so we can watch it when I fuck you later. Think about how full you'll be." Eddie eased the tip of his thumb in, too. God, he was so tempted, but fisting was something they would have to talk about when they weren't both horny as hell. He moved his thumb aside. "You'd be stuffed like never before, and when I take my hand out, your asshole would be open, waiting for my dick."

Damn it. That was more than he could handle. "I gotta fuck you."

"Yes," Carter hissed.

Eddie carefully extracted his fingers. He'd stashed condoms under the edge of the couch too, and in short order he had his penis sheathed and was sinking it into Carter's ass.

Eddie dropped down over Carter, holding him. "Jack yourself, baby. This is gonna be quick." They were both too turned on for it not to be.

Carter got his hand under him and soon his arm was moving in the tell-tale way of a man beating off. Eddie put both of his hands on Carter's nape and began hammering into his ass.

Carter's muscles gripped Eddie's cock just like they'd done with his fingers. It was intoxicatingly arousing to be buried in any part of Carter's body.

Eddie held him down and fucked him until Carter shuddered and came. When Carter's arm stopped moving, Eddie let go of Carter's nape and pulled his cock out of Carter's hole.

It took no time at all to whip off the condom. Eddie stroked himself off in three pulls, his cum splattering on Carter's back.

"I'm going to pass out one of these days. Those are some majorly intense orgasms," Carter said later, when they'd moved to the bed.

"True. And the same goes. It just keeps getting better between us."

Carter rolled onto his stomach and looked at Eddie. "If it works out with Dare, that's not going to change."

"No, it won't. I think maybe you ought to call him and talk to him, make dinner plans that will work for us all." Eddie liked the idea of Carter and Dare planning the whole deal. "I'd say we could invite him out here and I'd cook, but that's a hell of a long drive." Eddie yawned so hard it was a miracle his jaws didn't come unhinged.

"Get some sleep. I'll see if Dare's awake, and if he is, I'll call him." Carter kissed Eddie's lips. "I love you."

"Love you too." Eddie was worn out and elated at the same time. It was nice. He was aware of Carter getting up and leaving the room. After that, all Eddie knew were dreams and sleep.

Chapter Nine

After having spent five days with Eddie, Carter had to go back to Odessa. He liked his accounting job just fine—it wasn't exciting or anything, but he had great benefits and an awesome boss, yet he started to think about career alternatives.

For one thing, he wanted more time with Eddie. But if he managed that somehow, and the relationship with Dare worked out, then he might not see Dare as often as they'd all like.

It was a mess trying to figure it all out. Carter used the three hour drive home to concentrate on the issue but was unable to come up with a resolution.

"Maybe I shouldn't be counting my men before they're snagged," he muttered, after he'd plopped down on his couch.

Carter's phone vibrated with a text from Eddie. He'd never known he was so gooey inside, so romantic. Half the time when he thought of Eddie, he expected to find little hearts and flowers floating around his head. Carter snickered at the image then replied to Eddie. On impulse, he texted Dare, too. Their conversation had gone mostly smoothly the other day once they both found their footing.

Dare was a tad awkward on the phone, which meant he was being genuine, since that's how he was in person. Carter found it endearing. He was looking forward to having Dare join them Wednesday for dinner.

Stretching from head to toes, Carter moaned when his back popped. He was pleasantly sore and sated. Eddie hadn't been around as much as he usually was when Carter was there, and the bobcat was still on the loose. Eddie had still found time for sex, and Carter had benefitted greatly from that.

Carter grinned when Dare texted him back. All Carter had asked was how he was doing. Dare had replied, though, which thrilled him more than it probably should have.

For a little while, Carter and Dare conversed through messaging, then it was Carter, Dare and Eddie in a group text. Carter hoped they were all becoming friends. He and Eddie had started out with sex but their friendship had grown from there.

Carter stood and stretched again. His back was bothering him, probably from sleeping wrong. Or maybe it was from the way Eddie had bent him like a pretzel a time or two. Yoga might help with his flexibility. Carter would look into it.

Carter froze in the doorway to his bedroom, his heart racing as he took in the place. Goosebumps covered his skin and sweat broke out on his forehead. Carter couldn't see anything obvious out of place, yet he knew someone else had been in there. Might still be in there, for all he knew, hiding under the bed or in the closet.

Or behind the door. That's where the bad guys hide in the movies. But surely – Carter shouted as the door was jostled. "No!" He tried to dart back into the hallway.

A ski masked figure leaped out and reached for him.

Carter stumbled over his own feet as he tried to avoid being grabbed.

"Fuck you!" he shouted, swinging hard with his right fist. He couldn't see features but knew he was being attacked by a man—the size, the strength, the big gloved hand blocking his swing—

Carter kicked and refused to be still. His opponent seemed to have more hands than humanly possible. Panic tried to edge out reason, but Carter had enough sense to know if he couldn't think he'd likely be killed. He needed to be both smart and violent.

The masked man hit him in the ribs. Carter's breath gushed out of him and he thought he might throw up. *Can't.* Hesitating wasn't an option nor was being sick. Carter stomped on one of his attacker's booted feet, slamming his heel right on top of it.

"Goddamn it!" the intruder roared. At the same time, he slapped Carter upside the head, making his ears ring.

Carter fought back with another stomp, a kick, punches and he would have bitten if he could have. He took more than a few more hits and slaps himself, and narrowly missed being kneed in the balls.

"Get the fuck out!" he found the breath to yell when he slammed his elbow into the other man's stomach. There was no softness there. Whoever was in the bedroom with him was built like the proverbial brick wall. Carter wasn't any slouch himself, but he didn't have abs like the ones he'd just decked.

Even so, it was an effective maneuver.

"Fucking tease," the man rasped. "This isn't over." He shoved Carter away, knocking him onto his ass, then ran out of the room.

Carter's head hit the wall when he fell. It hurt, but then again, all of him hurt now. He forced himself to his feet and to give pursuit to no avail. The few seconds he'd been down had allowed the assailant to escape. Carter heard the door slam before he even managed two steps.

"God...damn," he panted, hunching over and holding his stomach. His ribs hurt like a mother, and so did most of the rest of him. Carter blinked at the closed door. What was he supposed to do now?

Cops. He needed to all them. Where was his phone? Carter couldn't quite stand up straight. He stumbled back to the bedroom. Right before the entrance, he stopped. There was no way he could go any farther. His nerves wouldn't let him.

Carter did see his phone, lying in the bedroom in about six different pieces.

"Aw, shit," he groaned. Now was one of the times people warned those who ditched landlines about. Carter had only used his cell. At least he had the important phone numbers in his contacts memorized, not that it did him any good. He couldn't call Eddie and let him know what happened.

And he couldn't call Dare. Carter took a shallow breath. He needed to call the police, and possibly an ambulance. Hopefully one of his neighbors would let him use their phone.

Carter was reaching for his front door when someone knocked on it. He went dizzy with fear then moved back. The door wasn't locked. *What if...?*

No, it made no sense for the attacker to come back. Carter had to force himself back to the door. He looked out the peephole as another knock sounded. Outside stood an elderly lady he'd seen once before. Carter had waved at her, and she'd waved back. He was pretty sure she was his neighbor to the left, though since he'd seen her at the mailboxes in the front of the complex, he could be wrong.

But she wasn't a complete stranger, or a masked man intent on hurting him, and Carter needed help. He stepped back and opened the door just a little, bracing his foot against it just in case.

"Oh. Oh my," the woman said, her voice shaking. "I'm Jerri. I live next door. I heard… Are you okay?"

Carter blinked. He hadn't been aware of how loud the fight must have been. Come to think of it, there had been a fist-sized hole in the wall by the door, or had he hallucinated that? It was just a flash of memory.

"Step out here and let me look at you. He's gone. I saw him leave. It's safe now," Jerri was saying.

"You saw him?" Carter asked, latching onto those words.

Jerri turned enough to point to the parking lot. "He ran out of your place. Slammed the door hard enough to rattle the windows, I'd bet, and got in a dark car over there.

She was pointing to an area of the lot where there was little to no light. The same area Carter had felt like someone was watching him from before.

"He's gone. He had on a black ski mask, so I don't know who he was. Not your boyfriend, I'd think. Wrong vehicle and I've never heard anything bad when your boyfriend visits."

Carter had a second to wonder just what she *had* heard when Eddie was staying over. God knew neither he nor Eddie were particularly quiet when fucking.

"You need the police, and you're bleeding," Jerri continued. "Have you called? I don't hear sirens. I'm not surprised your other neighbors didn't call them or come check on you. People now days don't care about others hardly at all."

"Carter," he said stupidly. "Hausemann. I'm Carter Hausemann."

Jerri smiled impishly, which smoothed out some of her wrinkles. "Well Carter Hausemann, I wish we'd have met under other circumstances. You look like you're about to keel over. Come with me. I can't imagine you'd want to stay in your apartment after being attacked there."

He didn't. "I couldn't call. My cell... It got broken."

Jerri sighed. "One of those without a real phone, eh? I hope you change that. Come on."

Carter squinted at her, confused as to why she was being nice.

"Don't look at me like that, young man. I was raised up in a time when people helped each other. Now come on and let's get you taken care of."

At the gentle scolding, Carter found himself moving. He stepped outside, closing the door behind him. He still couldn't stand up straight.

"Take my arm," Jerri offered, holding her right one out to him.

She was several inches shorter than him, and she was old. He started to tell her it was okay. The glare she gave him had Carter keeping quiet. He put a hand on her arm and made sure to keep his weight off it.

They shuffled over to her place. Jerri wasn't moving much faster than him just then. She might have been going slower for his sake, but Carter doubted it. He had seen her at the mailboxes, after all.

It wasn't far at all to her apartment, since it was right next door. The irrational fear that Jerri was in on the crime against him hit Carter before they went into her place. He gasped, unable to take another step.

"We're almost there," Jerri urged.

Carter's chest was tight. His fingers and toes went numb. Some part of his brain screamed *panic attack!* He couldn't make himself move.

"Carter, you have to come in, otherwise I'll have to leave you outside, alone, while I fetch the phone." Jerri patted his hand. "Take a very deep breath, hold it then let it out slowly. Do that until it doesn't feel like an elephant is sitting on your chest."

Jerri's pronouncement cut through Carter's spinning thoughts. He tried to take a deep breath. The first attempt left him coughing.

"Try again. My Tom used to have panic attacks after he got back from the war. You'll move past it."

Her kindness made his eyes burn with unshed tears. Carter got a good breath in, and after following Jerri's advice, was able to calm himself.

"Thank you," he got out, still feeling entirely too close to breaking down and sobbing. Carter hated feeling so weak. He wanted anger, a raging fury, rather than what he was dealing with emotionally.

"You'll do fine." She patted his hand again. "Let me just get the door."

After Jerri helped him inside, she handed him a cordless phone. "Call whoever you need to. I'd suggest the cops and ambulance first. You're hunched like your ribs are hurt. Then maybe that boyfriend of yours?"

"Eddie." God, Carter wanted to call him first.

"He's a nice-looking young man. I always did have a thing for a man on a motorcycle." Jerri waved a hand dismissively. "Make your calls and never mind me. I'll babble all evening."

Carter dialed emergency services. He gave a brief recounting of what happened and told the dispatcher that yes, he might need an ambulance. He refused to stay on the line with him, though. Calling Eddie was the priority at that point.

"Hello?" Eddie sounded remote, not like the warm, loving man Carter knew him to be.

Carter was stricken with chills just that suddenly. His teeth chattered and he tried to get Eddie's name out to no avail?

"Who is this?" Eddie demanded. "Is—?"

Jerri pried the phone away from him. "Hello, Eddie. This is Carter's neighbor Jerri. He's been assaulted."

Carter squeaked out a protest at the blunt announcement. Jerri ignored him. Eddie bellowed loud enough that Jerri held the phone away from her ear.

"I can't tell you anything if you won't top hollering," she shouted into the phone. It must have quieted Eddie down, because she was able to recount part of Carter's tale, the basics of it, in a matter of moments.

"He's here, and the police and ambulance are on the way." Jerri was silent as she looked Carter over. "He's hurt. I don't know how bad. Hunched like his stomach or ribs are messed up. Has a split lip and one and a half black eyes. A half because the other's not fully black, that's why. I'd have thought you'd be brighter than that."

Carter heard buzzing in his ears and closed his eyes. He wasn't going to panic again, or pass out.

"Talk to him," Jerri said.

Carter felt her press the phone to his ear. "Carter, honey, I'm on the way. I'll be on the road in three minutes flat. I'm going to call Dare, if that's okay. He can get to you quickly. Unless you don't want me to."

"I-I don't know." Carter was confused and scared, and hurting bad enough that the pain was interfering with everything else. "Trust you," he got out, meaning he was fine with whatever Eddie decided. Carter just wanted the hurting to stop and to erase the events of the last fifteen minutes.

"I'll call him. You shouldn't be alone at the hospital. I love you, Carter. You're going to be okay. How bad do you feel?"

"Like shit," he scraped out. "Hurry."

Eddie sucked in a sharp breath Carter could hear over the phone. "How bad?"

"I'll live. I think it's superficial," Carter forced himself to say. "But I want you."

"I'll be there. Can I speak to Jerri again?"

"Love you," Carter told him then handed the phone to Jerri. He could hear the blare of sirens and what was left of his strength was fading fast.

"I'll let you know what hospital they take him to. You're sending a friend to sit with him? I can't go to the hospital. Oh good. You're a good man."

Carter agreed whole-heartedly.

One minute he was standing, leaning against the wall, and the next he was surrounded by EMT's. Carter couldn't recall what happened, but his head pounded as hard as his ribs.

"Hey, buddy. You passed out and Mrs. Corrigan couldn't catch you. On top of everything else, you did a number on your noggin'." The EMT smiled at him.

Carter found it easier to let his eyes close and drift. The next time he woke up, he was in a hospital bed and a sort of familiar face was peering down at him.

"Oh!" Dare leaned back.

Carter had to blink several times before he could see clearly. One of his eyes was definitely not cooperating. He started to reach up and touch it.

"I wouldn't do that," Dare said, touching Carter's forearm lightly. "Your left eye is swollen shut. It looks like it must hurt a lot."

"Does," Carter said. The word came out odd.

"Busted lips," Dare informed him with a nod. "You don't need stitches. Eddie should be here soon. You've been out for almost two hours. I don't think the doctors were happy about that at *all* since you have a head injury. Got stitches back there, but that's the only place. I think you should be getting the results of the CT scan back soon."

Carter cautiously licked his lips. His mouth and throat were very dry, which was as bad as the hurting had been. That, at least, was dulled for now, either by drugs or something else. He didn't know or care, as long as he wasn't one big, throbbing raw nerve.

Dare fidgeted with the sheet by Carter's arm. "I was... Um. I was surprised to be called, I guess." He flitted a glance at Carter's face then went back to fiddling with the sheet. "I don't really know what to do."

Carter wished they hadn't been pushed together. He didn't mind it, nor did he think Eddie had been wrong necessarily to call Dare. Carter sure was glad he hadn't woken up alone. But Dare seemed uncomfortable, and that made Carter regret him being there—for Dare's sake.

Dare wanted to hug Carter, actually, though it didn't look like there wasn't many places on him that weren't bruised. He'd seen Carter's chest and stomach, his sides and even the tops of his thighs when one of the nurses had come in to check the injuries. Carter had been beaten up, for sure. Dare didn't know the way of it. He'd only gotten that terse call from Eddie.

Oh, Eddie hadn't been rude, but he'd been very brief and Dare could understand why. Being three hours away when your boyfriend was attacked had to suck.

What Dare couldn't figure out was his place there. Then again, he and the other two men hadn't had time to get to know each other or anything. He supposed he should just sit back and see what happened.

"You didn't ring to let me know he was awake!"

Carter tried to turn his head and groaned. Dare sank down a little in his seat as the nurse, a scowling woman by the name of Cindy, came in.

"I didn't. I thought the monitors would—" Good Lord, he was a successful business owner, not a scared kid. He sat up straighter again. "Isn't that why the monitors are there? And don't they go off at your station or something like that?"

Cindy could've scared a raging bull with the glare she leveled at him. "I wasn't at the desk to see the readouts and nothing went off. He's awake. His vitals aren't much different, and I'd have liked to know he was finally coming to."

Dare decided to quit arguing with her. He was out of sorts anyway. He hated hospitals and doctor's offices, a hang up from when he had cancer. At the same time, he was grateful for them, too, because they saved lives, his included. Still, it gave him the heebie-jeebies to be in a hospital again.

Then there was the attraction he felt for the man in the hospital bed. It shouldn't have affected Dare so much. His heart ached a little and he'd had a few tears slip out, despite his best effort to restrain them. The idea that this happened to Carter at the same time they'd all been texting, that unsettled Dare.

There were lots of what-ifs, too—enough that he was almost certain he was going to have to give this thing with the three of them a shot. Because the biggest what-if—*what if Carter had been killed?*—really bothered Dare. That told him he was already somehow, sort of, invested in Carter and Eddie both.

If he lost Carter, he'd lose Eddie too.

Maybe that wouldn't be the case if the relationship worked out, and one of them… Well, he wasn't going down that depressing as all get-out road.

Dare watched the nurse checking Carter.

"I'm going to have to remove the piercing," she said, gesturing to his chest.

The knowledge that Carter had pierced nipples went right to Dare's cock and it tried to firm up. Dare silently scolded his unruly part. Now was not the time for his pecker to be getting involved.

"You have a concussion, stitches in the back of your scalp, and bruised ribs. Your left eye is swollen shut, and you have busted lips. A few other bruises that are going to hurt over the next week or so, but it's mainly the ribs that will give you trouble." Cindy put a finger to her lips. "Shh, don't tell that I let you know about your ribs. The doctor is the one who's supposed to give you those results. She's been in surgery and will be there for several hours still, so I thought I'd ease your mind a little. The police are going to want to talk to you now that you're awake. I'll have to get them out of the cafeteria, I bet. We have donuts there."

That almost got a laugh out of Dare. He wouldn't have thought the nurse had a sense of humor. Perhaps he shouldn't have been so judgmental. Everything was just…weird right now, including him and he needed to watch himself. Kindness was something Dare strived to exude every day. It wasn't easy. Some days he failed and said something he regretted, but he was getting better about that.

To that end, when Nurse Cindy started to leave, Dare stopped her. He hopped up and she arched an eyebrow at him.

"I apologize for my tone and words. I honestly didn't know I was supposed to call."

Cindy's expression went from irritated to a smile that was startlingly pretty. "It's all right. I shouldn't have snapped either. It's been a long day."

"Well, I couldn't do what you do," he told her. "Thank you."

She tipped her head at him. "I'll be sending those cops in when they get here. You might want to be careful what you say with them. One of them, Dennis, he's a friend of my brother's and I've heard some of the crap he spews off the clock."

"Thanks," Dare said. Sometimes he hated the world he lived in. He silently chastised himself for that thought. Letting ignorant people ruin his positivity was stupid and he wouldn't give them such power.

Dare sat back in his seat. He was careful not to cross his legs or move his hands much, nothing he thought might make him appear to be a stereotype for Detective Dennis.

The police arrived a few minutes later, a man who had to be the one he'd been warned about, and a woman who gave him a brief smile. Dare introduced himself and said that he was a friend who'd only met

Carter a short while ago through the tour at his microbrewery.

The sideways squint Detective Dennis had been giving him lightened up. "You're that Dare? From Dare's Microbrews?"

As tempting as it was to be sarcastic, Dare refrained. "Yes, I am. You should come for a tour sometime. Complimentary, both of you," he nodded to the other Detective, "And a guest, if you'd like." He hoped he hadn't just broken some law by offering.

Detective Dennis beamed at him. "I'd love to. Janie," he turned to his partner, "You think your husband would like to go with us? I can ask Abby and we'll make it a double date."

"Sure," Janie agreed. "And thank you, Mr. Habrock. Now, should we do our jobs, you think?"

Detective Dennis began questioning Carter. Dare felt really bad for the poor man, trying to answer questions when his lips were swollen.

Cindy came in to give him some ice chips, which seemed to help some. Dare just tried to stay out of the way and not come off as gay to Dennis.

He'd make sure someone else gave that tour.

As Dare listened to Carter's halting recounting of the attack, his own problems faded away. Instead a ball of hot worry began to build in his gut. He hadn't known Carter thought he was being stalked. That's what it sounded like at least.

Carter couldn't describe the attacker, or say if he sounded like the same man he'd worked with who'd been fixated on him.

"My ears were ringing, and I was panicking," Carter admitted. "I don't remember how he sounded."

Eventually, the detectives left. Dare told them to call and let Dee know when they wanted to come in.

"Could I have more ice?" Carter asked.

"Of course." Dare used the call button to request some. "They shouldn't take long, I'd hope."

The nurse on duty was quick. She came into the room, a nice smile in place. "Here you go. If you need anything else, don't hesitate to call for me." She handed Dare the cup and spoon.

Dare took them and smiled back, though it felt forced on his part. "Thanks." He moved his chair closer to Carter then. It seemed very intimate to be sitting there slipping tiny slivers of ice between Carter's lips. Carter stared at him with that one, not swollen shut eye. Dare wasn't sure if he should look there or at both eyes or what. He felt awkward, yet drawn to help. Drawn to Carter.

And a few minutes later, when Eddie strode in, worry pinching his attractive features, Dare's heart did a flop and he knew there was something there too. Eddie gave him a hug.

"Thanks, Dare. Thanks for being here."

Dare didn't know where to put his hands or if he could, or should, hug Eddie back. *This is stupid. They want — wanted — more from me. It's okay to hug him.* He got in a quick one then stepped back, figuring Eddie would want to see Carter.

"You're welcome." Dare was prepared to feel left out from then on. He didn't. Eddie included him in the conversation and he asked Dare what had happened, since Carter had difficulty speaking clearly. It was part of why the police interview had taken so long.

Dare eventually had to leave. He wasn't used to being away from work or home much. "I'll... Let me know how Carter's doing?" Dare asked of Eddie.

Eddie studied him for a second or two. "I'd still like you to have dinner with us."

"I'd like that too." Dare really would. He left feeling strangely optimistic, considering Carter was hurt. The optimism wasn't in conjunction with that. For the first time in many years, he felt ready to take a chance — daring, even, much like the shortened form of his name, Darren.

He refused to dwell on the things he was insecure about. They weren't going away any time soon, but he didn't have to give them headroom.

So he went home and showered, and let himself imagine what might happen between the men he'd hopefully be having dinner with. Dare kept his little fantasies clean, since it seemed wrong to have dirty ones with Carter in the hospital turning various shades of black, blue and purple.

They were still good fantasies. He was beginning to think they could really make it work.

Chapter Ten

Eddie had forgotten to call his mom. That wouldn't have been such a big concern if she hadn't left him a voicemail informing him of her choice of hotels—which wasn't a hotel at all, but rather his RV. When he slipped out of Carter's room to return her call, Eddie didn't give her a chance to tear him a new one. He started off telling her Carter had been attacked and from there, that she needed to understand he wasn't going to be at his RV and Carter sure wasn't ready for company.

"But he has his mom?" she asked. "She's going to help?"

Lying had never been such a temptation. Eddie wouldn't stoop to that level. "His mom died a long time ago. Carter doesn't have any family, and maybe you can see why you popping up might be too much for him right now." Eddie took a second to calm himself, because his next words, though yet unspoken, were on the tip of his tongue and making him angry. "Mom, he doesn't even want to go back to his place. I can't blame him. The cops haven't got a clue who did this to him." That was the truth. No one knew where Mark was, and Carter couldn't say for certain if it had been Mark's voice he heard. "He just wants some comfort, and I can do that for him."

She sighed and he knew he'd won this particular battle.

"Fine, son. If you or Carter needs anything, let us know. We'll help how we can. Tino hasn't found out anything, he said."

"No, he hasn't." Eddie finished the call up and returned to Carter's hospital room.

Carter's left eye was open some now, two days after the assault. "Can you check on my release papers?"

"Sure I can. I'll be right back." Eddie knew Carter was eager to get out of the hospital. They'd agreed on a decent hotel in Odessa for a few nights. After that, decisions would have to be made. Carter had another week off from work. Eddie didn't, though if he had been married to a wife, he could have taken leave.

He and Carter weren't married at all, and if they ever wanted to be, it'd mean going to another state to do it. For the first time, Eddie really started thinking about the reasons marriage—and a transfer—might be a wise decision.

But there was Dare, who'd come to see Carter daily and called or texted Eddie to check on them both. Did he want to walk away from Dare without seeing if the three of them could make something special?

Should he put that in front of Carter? Then again, for all he knew, Carter wouldn't want to leave his job—or Texas.

Damn it. They all needed to talk. Somehow he'd gotten closer to Dare in the past few days, and so had Carter. It was happening fairly quickly between them, perhaps because of the scare they'd all experienced.

Carter's elderly neighbor, Jerri, had let Eddie know when the police had come and gone from Carter's apartment. She seemed to be a new friend too and if Carter needed mothering, Eddie suspected Jerri would shove his mom out of the way for a chance at it.

As Eddie walked down to the nurses' station, he tried to work out some of the questions. It wasn't possible for him to do it alone. Maybe when Carter had a few days rest away from the hospital where he was being poked and prodded and tested for everything in the world, maybe then they could sit down and talk—the three of them.

The nurse at the station was the one who seemed to like him—Cindy. Eddie offered her a smile.

She was onto him. "He's nagging you to get him out, right?"

"You know Carter well," Eddie agreed.

Cindy giggled, and Dr. Elizondo came around the corner just then. "He's wanting these, I bet," she said, waving a stack of papers in the air. "We're heading there now. I've already sent an orderly for a wheelchair."

"Thanks." They walked back to the room, and Eddie paid attention to every detail of what Dr. Elizondo told him to do for Carter's aftercare. He thanked her and Cindy.

The orderly arrived pushing the wheelchair. He helped Carter get into the chair, then handed it over to Eddie once they were outside the hospital.

"I need to bring the truck around."

Carter tried to glance over his shoulder. The bald patch where he'd been shaved for the stitches made Eddie want to beat someone.

No, he wouldn't do that. He wasn't like the asshole who'd hurt Carter.

"The orderly is watching. Damn it. I can walk."

Eddie caressed the top of Carter's hair. "I'd rather you just wait here and I think he has to make sure you leave the hospital without getting hurt."

Carter raised a hand and self-consciously covered his bald spot. "I look horrible. This is awful."

"It's just hair. It'll grow back." Eddie understood pride well, however. "If you want, we could get it evened out."

Carter's expression showed astonishment. "You mean...totally bald?"

"You'd be sexy as f—" Eddie noticed the family hurrying past him and Carter. "You know what," he finished with.

"You do it."

Eddie thought Carter meant for him to shave his own hair off. "Me?"

Carter cackled. "Should see your face. I meant you shave it off for me, not shave yours off. I don't want to go get it done. I just want to hide."

"For a few days," Eddie temporized. Carter couldn't hide forever. "I'll be right back." He gestured the orderly over. "I'll be right back."

"We'll be here," the man said.

Eddie hurried to his truck. He hoped it didn't jostle Carter too much, though it likely would. He should have called a cab or asked Dare if he had a smoother riding vehicle for this.

The first thing Eddie noticed was the long, deep scratch down the side of the truck. "Motherfucker," he snarled, jogging over to it. On the driver's side door, it was worse. *You're dead*, the damage there proclaimed. Eddie looked around. No one suspicious was out, and there were no cameras in the lot. "Of course there isn't. Motherfucker," he grumbled again. He was going to have to call the police who were working Carter's case. They needed to be the ones taking the report.

Then there was Carter. He didn't want to stress him out. He also wouldn't be able to keep this from him. Eddie made two calls. The first was to leave a voicemail asking Detective Dennis to contact him. The second was to order a taxi.

Eddie returned to Carter and smiled rigidly, knowing Carter would see through but hoping the orderly wouldn't. "Battery's dead. A taxi is on the way."

"That sucks, man."

Eddie made a sound of agreement. Carter frowned. Eddie just said, "Soon."

Carter didn't wave at the taxi this time, and it saddened Eddie. He was being silly. Carter was released, and they could spend some time together before Eddie had to return to his job.

They helped Carter into the taxi. Eddie slid in the other side and read off the address for the hotel. Fortunately, their cabbie wasn't chatty.

"What happened?" Carter asked in a low voice.

Eddie took one of Carter's hands and held it. The driver could fuck off if he didn't like it. "Keyed. There were words on the driver's door. A threat."

Carter paled so much Eddie feared he'd pass out. "What did it say?"

Speaking two words shouldn't be so difficult, yet they hung in Eddie's throat.

"Eddie, what did they say?"

"You're dead," he blurted out. "And I've got a call in to Detective Dennis. I just didn't want to say anything in front of the orderly." He leaned closer to Carter.

"We're going to get the bastard, Carter. He's not going to win."

Carter shivered.

"I mean it," Eddie reiterated. "I'll use him for bobcat bait if I can."

"We should warn Dare," Carter muttered. "He's not going to want anything to do with us, and maybe that's for the best."

"We do need to warn him. You're right. I hope he won't run, but I'll let him know there'll be no hard feelings if he does." Eddie took his phone out. "Maybe I should wait until we're at the hotel."

"Thanks for that. I don't want to go back to that place." Another shudder rocked Carter. "I understand now why Mom was scared to leave her house."

"But—"

"But this happened in my home," Carter said. "So where am I safe? Where can I go that I won't feel like I'm being watched, like I'm prey for some man who is unhinged? Is there a place?"

There was, and Eddie had only just thought of it. "You could go to Albuquerque. My mom's been nagging me again about meeting you, and you'd never be alone. Even at night, because I bet one of the dogs would be claiming part of your bed."

"I can't. That's too much. I don't know them. It'd be imposing and frankly, the idea scares me almost as much as going back to the apartment does." Carter closed his eyes. "I don't know what to do."

"Right now, we're going to get out and go to this very nice hotel I've been staying in. We're going to relax, and order room service if we get hungry. I'll call Dare, fill him in on what's happening. If he doesn't want to give up on us, I'll ask if he wants to come over. Maybe *he* can shave your head, because I'm afraid I'll screw it up."

Carter snorted. "How can you mess up making someone completely bald?"

"I'd do it somehow."

The cabbie pulled up to the front of the hotel. Eddie took some money out of his pocket and paid for the fare and tip. "Have a good one." He got out then moved around to the other side to assist Carter.

"At least we don't have to check in," Carter said. "People are going to stare."

"Ah, see, one of the bellhops is a really nice lady named Zoe. I told her a little bit about what happened—just that you'd been hurt," Eddie clarified, lest Carter think he'd said more. "She is waiting to take us up in the staff elevators."

"Good afternoon, Mr. Canales, Mr. Hausemann," a young lady called out. Her sunny disposition fairly rolled off her in waves. "I'm Zoe, Mr. Hausemann, and I've got this under control."

"Thank you." Carter offered a weak smile that still stretched his poor split lips.

"It's my pleasure." Zoe led them inside and behind the front desk. They avoided most customers and the employees were polite enough not to gawk. Zoe stopped at the elevator. She pressed the Up button. "Here you go. Mr. Canales, do you want me to accompany you?"

"We're good, thanks." He tipped her then slipped an arm around Carter. "This isn't as nice as the other elevators. Figured it doesn't matter."

"It doesn't," Carter said.

The elevator opened up. They got on. "You wanna press the button?" Eddie asked. "Floor three."

Carter probably rolled his eyes in a fit of humor. "I'm not a kid. Have at it."

Eddie had always argued with his brothers and sisters over who got to punch the buttons in elevators. They'd been way older than they should have been before they'd stopped. He pressed the right button. "Got us a nice room. I also picked up your mail last night and brought it back there for when you were released today. Checked on Jerri. She's something, you know?"

The elevator stopped. They exited once the doors opened. "Room's right down here." Eddie had one on the end. He took out the key card. "First night I was here, I put the card in my pocket with the phone. You know what that can do to a key card?"

"Wipe it clean so it doesn't work," Carter said. "Been there, was locked out to prove it."

"Least I'm not the only one." One swipe and Eddie was able to open the door. "After you, honey."

Carter entered, looking so weary and bruised Eddie ached for him. "This is nice." Carter went right to the large window that made up an entire wall. "They need to have something spectacular out there instead of the city. Mountains, trees..."

Eddie could have pointed out that Carter was in the wrong area for both of those things. There was no need to.

Carter turned and started shuffling over to the bed. "I need to lie down. I hate being so fucking weak."

"You're not weak," Eddie all but snapped. "You're hurt, and you'll get better. Now, let me get you one of your pain pills. After you take it, I'll step out—"

"Stay," Carter pleaded. "Don't...don't leave me alone."

Eddie walked over to the counter where Carter's medicines were. "Okay, I won't. You need to rest, and I need to call Dare—and I have to see if I can get a rental car delivered here. We can't be without a vehicle. I can do that in the bathroom so I don't keep you up."

"You won't. I've been in the hospital with all the beeping and yakking. I can promise you that I'll be asleep before my head hits the pillow."

Eddie fished a pain pill from the bottle. He settled the lid on the container. "There still a bottle of water by the bed?" He couldn't remember seeing it.

"Yeah." Carter sank down onto the bed. "God, you have no idea how good this feels."

"Unfortunately I do, since the nurses wouldn't let me spend the night up there with you. They chased me off."

Carter held his hand out. "Threatened to call security. I heard."

Eddie came over. He put the pill in Carter's hand.

Carter popped the medicine in his mouth. He followed it up with a swig of water.

Eddie's brain kicked out something—all on its own, he'd have sworn—without giving him a chance to rethink it. "You know, if we were married—"

"Jesus," Carter wheezed, water dripping from his chin.

"We could, in New Mexico," Eddie continued. He'd already started down that road anyway. "Maybe not right now, or you know, if things work out with Dare, one of us should be married to another one of us. The hospitals and doctors would have to honor that."

Carter pressed a hand to his chest. He gasped a few times, then picked something up off his lap. "Gross." It was the pill, and it was lumpy. Carter put it in his mouth and swallowed it down before Eddie could offer to get him another one.

Eddie kept his mouth shut while Carter took a drink this time.

Carter put the bottle down on the stand by the bed. "I get what you're aiming for, Eddie. It's something we should discuss later, when we know…"

Whether or not Dare – or another man – will be a part of us. Eddie nodded. "You're right. Wouldn't hurt to have legal docs drawn up, whatever ones we can have and use."

"No, it wouldn't." Carter snuffled and carefully laid back. "I appreciate the proposal. No one's ever wanted to marry me before." A smile tipped one corner of his mouth.

Eddie watched him fall asleep between one breath and the next.

He still headed for the bathroom, hoping to keep from disturbing Carter. There were no missed calls from anyone, so he reckoned the police would get back to him in their own sweet time. "Yeah right." Fuck that, he'd call the other detective after he spoke to Dare.

He arranged to have a decent sized car brought to the hotel for him to use. His truck would be painted in a rush job since he had to get back to Big Bend in a few days. Eddie could deal with driving a sedan until then.

That handled, he relaxed a little and finally called Dare.

Chapter Eleven

As Dare drove over to the hotel, he wondered if it wouldn't be wiser to turn around and go back to his lonely life. His mother, though he loved her, wasn't enough to keep him from sinking into the pits of single-sap despair at times. Then he'd get all morose and worry about dying alone. Boy, he was a barrel of laughs during those times.

The thing was, he was sure those periods of depression—that's what he thought they were—would only get worse if he *did* give up now. He and Carter and Eddie already had a tenuous bond between the three of them. Could he turn tail and run because someone might key his car?

"No." *But what if they hurt me? Is it worth that risk? What if I die?*

"What if I never live?" he asked under his breath. Hadn't he been hiding away since the cancer treatments? At least from having a romantic relationship? He'd dated a few men here and there, but never let it progress past a few kisses. He'd been too embarrassed about his bony, flawed body. If Hank hadn't dumped him shortly after the disease was found... He had, however. And he'd said some hateful, awful things, whether Hank had considered them such or not.

They'd marked Dare on his soul for all these years. Eddie and Carter made him want to move past that damage. As to the other, he'd have to deal with it. He wasn't the only man walking around wounded, and it was past time for him to let the pain and fear go.

Dare let the valets handle parking his car. He headed into the hotel and went right to the bank of elevators. It seemed to take forever for one to reach the lobby floor. A small herd of people exited. Dare wondered how the elevator hadn't gotten stuck.

There were a few people that rode up with him, though only he got off on the third floor. Dare checked the plaque on the wall with the room numbers and arrows on it. He went in the direction of room three-ten. It was at the end of the hall, and he knocked softly on the door.

Eddie opened it almost instantly. "Come in. Carter's still sleeping, but he's likely to wake soon."

Dare entered, and Eddie surprised him by brushing a chaste kiss over Dare's cheek. The gentle buss was more than Dare had gotten from a man in a while and it went through his body like a wildfire spurred on by the wind.

"I'm glad you decided not to ditch us." Eddie took his hand. "Carter will be, too. If you do change your mind, we won't be assholes about it."

"I don't think I will," Dare murmured, keeping an eye on Carter, who while still bruised but appeared to be more comfortable than he had since he'd been hurt. "Did you get a hold of one of the cops?"

"Yeah, I did. Dennis called me back as I was dialing his partner's number. He's already taken the report and pictures of the damage. My insurance company will be on it, too. An adjuster is supposed to go to the garage I had the truck towed to." Eddie seemed proud of himself as he added, "I got a lot done in the past couple of hours, including finding an actual towing company that's listed as LGBT-friendly. The wonders of the Internet."

"It's a great tool. My business wouldn't be half what it is without the 'Net." Dare took a seat on the small couch by the window. "Is there anything I can do to help?" He got a little jittery when Eddie sat beside him. The man was just big — and muscle-y — and Dare's cock always wanted to come out and play when Eddie or Carter got close to him. "Um."

"Do I make you nervous," Eddie asked, "or horny?"

Dare just knew he was three shades of red. His face and neck were hot. He was blushing, damn it all. "H-horny."

Eddie's lips kicked into a grin. "Good. That's what I was hoping for."

Dare bobbed his head, agreeing with what, he hadn't a clue.

"Can I kiss you, then, Dare?" Eddie asked. "While Carter watches us?"

Dare jerked his gaze over to find Carter watching them intently. "I... Yes?"

Carter propped himself up.

Eddie cupped Dare's chin. "Don't look so scared. I won't bite. Yet."

Dare couldn't for the life of him have repressed the shiver that went through his body. "This matters," he said, needing Eddie and Carter both to know it.

"It does, or neither of us would be interested." Eddie dipped his head down and lightly rubbed his mouth over Dare's.

"He kisses like a dream, Dare. Trust me — and Eddie."

At Carter's prompting, Dare let himself go, casting off his fears, at least for a little while.

Eddie whispered that Dare was a good man. He licked Dare's lip and moved his other hand around to hold Dare at the back of his head.

Then he did it. Eddie kissed him like Dare had always dreamed a man should be kissed. Strong, tender, demanding — taking, and giving at the same time.

Dare's cock was erect in seconds as he tried to get closer to Eddie. He'd forgotten this, the heat between two bodies, the lust and need. What would it be like with three of them?

Dare was suddenly, acutely ravenous for more. He whimpered when Eddie rumbled and pushed his tongue in deep, laying claim to Dare's mouth. Dare ran his hands over the bulging biceps and triceps. He ached to come.

Eddie pressed him back. Dare went, winding up with his head on the arm of the couch, his legs hanging off the other end, and Eddie kneeling between his spread thighs, one arm braced on the back of the couch while kissing him still.

Dare was in heaven. Eddie stroked his chest and tugged on his nipples. Dare didn't like pain, and Eddie seemed to know when to let up on his nubs before it became too much.

Then Eddie's hand was one Dare's belt and that cold ball of fear that had snuck off for a while came slamming back into Dare. He twisted his head aside. "Wait, wait," he begged. "I can't. I can't."

Eddie's chest was heaving as he pushed himself up until he was on his knees and off Dare. "It's cool. Dare, it's fine."

Dare hadn't realized he was still babbling and grabbing at his belt as if to keep it fastened. He forced himself to press his lips together until they hurt.

Eddie ran a hand through his hair. Dare couldn't look him in the eyes any more than he could meet Carter's gaze. He was ashamed of his meltdown.

"It's really okay, Dare." Eddie touched his leg, right above the knee.

Dare didn't flinch. He wasn't worried about his leg.

"That's the rule with any lover. Always stop if they want you to. Neither of us would push you, Dare."

Dare wondered if Eddie kept using his name in an attempt to sort of ground him. It was working. Dare wasn't so close to running away.

"Did someone hurt you?" Carter asked in a quiet voice.

Dare thought of Hank and his cruel words. That wasn't what Carter meant, he realized. Dare had to speak up before Carter and Eddie got the wrong idea. "No," he got out. "Not like that." Dare closed his eyes. He needed courage, and it was stupid—so stupid to be so scared of sex.

No, not of sex. Of being seen.

"You don't have to explain." Eddie kept caressing him. "This moves at your pace."

That forced a bitter laugh from Dare. It also freed his tongue. "Then it might be another decade before I have sex again. I don't want that."

"A—" Carter cleared his throat, but his voice still squeaked when he added, "*another* decade?"

Dare wanted to crawl under the couch. He didn't. He was coming to realize how much he really did care for the two men watching him. Dare raised his head. He glanced from Carter to Eddie. "I told you I had testicular cancer. I had a partner at the time, a man I'd been with for years. Three years." At least the pain of Hank's abandonment had ceased. "Hank was freaked out by the diagnosis. He said he'd be there for me regardless. Then we learned I'd have to have surgery."

Carter hissed like an overheated teapot. Eddie growled.

Dare felt marginally better. "Yes. He...said some things about me being unattractive. I'd always been thin but with the cancer, I lost my appetite. I was terrified, and Hank wasn't being as supportive as he'd claimed. I found out he was cheating on me."

"What an asshole," Carter mumbled.

"He was. When I confronted him days after the surgery to have my...my right testicle removed, he told me he'd just started the affair because he had to get laid with someone he found attractive. He wasn't interested in someone deformed like I was. He said even a prosthetic would still be weird." Dare wrung his hands. "I know. I know he was being a heartless bastard. He was lashing out at me because he was caught cheating, which he'd been doing for almost a year, I later learned. It didn't matter. I had loved him and he hurt me."

"We won't, not ever," Eddie said. "Carter and me, we aren't superficial jerks. We know this is unconventional, but it's genuine. It's not about sex, though sure, that's a part of it. It's about loving as much as we can. We have room for you, Dare."

"We do," Carter agreed. "We want you, and we care about you."

Dare wiped at the sweat on his brow. The room wasn't warm, but he was so nervous, and he wasn't done yet. "I didn't want the prosthetic testicle. Maybe it would have made me feel better about myself later on. All I could think was, it was something unnatural in my body. You get crazy thoughts sometimes when you're seriously ill. I feared putting anything like that in my body. I went to extremes with juice diets that promised to cleanse out cancer cells and lost even more weight. It was a bad time in more ways than one."

"I think I understand that. I'm terrified to go back to my apartment, to be alone, even. My mother... She was mentally ill. She was a germaphobe. I'm pretty sure she had mysophobia, though she never was diagnosed with it. Our house was spotless and always smelled like cleaning chemicals. I wasn't allowed outside or around other kids the older I got, because her illness grew stronger." Carter sighed. "I was so angry at her about it even after she died, but now I wish I'd asked her if something bad happened to her, too. Now I understand the depth of the fear she felt, even if I'm not there where she was. I understand overreacting when fear for your life is involved, and our brains take a long time to process that fear and deal with it."

Eddie watched them both with affection and perhaps regret, Dare wasn't sure.

"I'm sorry both of you know what that's like," Eddie said. He rubbed Dare's arm. "You are both stronger than I am."

Dare snorted at that but Carter didn't. He only murmured, "There are different kinds of strength, Dare."

"And as for us three, we can support each other and have something amazing that suits us all." Eddie kept stroking Dare's arm.

It was a simple touch, nonsexual, even, yet Dare had trouble concentrating. It'd been so long since anyone had touched him in a way that wasn't platonic or familial. Still, he got his act together. There were things to be discussed. "But how will it work?"

Eddie got off the couch. "Let's sit with Carter, okay?" He extended a hand to Dare.

Dare took it then let himself be helped up. It wasn't just his legs that were shaky. All of him jangled. He walked with Eddie over to the bed.

Carter patted the middle of the mattress. "Here?"

Dare had to let go of Eddie's hand to go back to the other side of the bed. He got on, then scooted to the middle so Eddie could get up as well.

"How do you want this to work?" Carter asked. "I've never done it before."

"Me either, not for more than a night," Eddie said.

Dare had known that. It had come up in conversation before, yet he'd somehow forgotten he wasn't the only one new at such a relationship.

"And you should know, Carter and I love each other, and we'll love you, too, if you give us a chance." Eddie rested a hand on Dare's stomach. Carter did, too.

"What if you don't? Or can't?" Dare asked, voicing one of his bigger fears. "I don't want to be loved second best."

"Dare," Carter said tenderly.

"It won't happen. We can love you, and that's why it will happen, if you want it to." Eddie edged closer. "Dare, you're an amazing guy. You're shy and smart, determined and sweet, and so sexy any man would be a fool to cheat on you. We want you, in our beds and in our lives."

"Where? I don't understand. You work in Big Bend, Carter's in Odessa. I'm here, too. How does it work?" he asked again. "Are we only together when you're here? I can't take off like Carter does for the weekends. I don't know anything about hiking, but I'd like to try it, if I can find the time."

"We can trust each other, be with whoever's around in a sexual way, or we can only have sex when we're all together. That'd be harder, but we'd do it."

Dare thought about Eddie's proposal. "That doesn't seem fair. I don't know how I'd deal with knowing you two were... It's different now—or has been up until now. I was still on the outside of what you have together. I can admit I might be petty, jealous. Insecure."

"That's all understandable," Carter assured him. "Especially after Hank cheated."

"And you know, I might be bothered too," Eddie said. "I like to watch if I'm not participating. I've been cheated on, and it was the lying that cut me a lot more than the physical part. I think maybe, if you both would be willing to video chat with me while you mess around, I'd feel included."

"What if you didn't? I wouldn't want to hurt you." Dare didn't want any of them to be hurt.

"So we try it once. It's turning me on to think about it, so I'm betting it'll be fine." Eddie cupped his bulging erection. "See? Not unhappy about the idea at all."

"We could keep it to blow jobs and hand jobs, too," Carter offered. "Until it's the three of us. Like now."

Oh, Carter was smooth. Dare's cock was going to burst right out of his jeans. "I don't like to...um...top..." he mumbled.

"Not a problem," Eddie said as Carter agreed. "Yeah, really not a problem. Eddie is a top through and through, I'm vers. We'll all work great together."

Dare clenched his buttocks. It'd been ages since he'd had a real dick in him. Still, there was more to discuss. "But when you're with Eddie in Big Bend—"

"Dare." Carter sat up, grimacing as he did so. "What days do you take off work?"

"None," he answered immediately. "I mean...almost never."

"Don't you think you could change that? Maybe designate some responsibility now and then?" Carter asked.

Dare had been considering it ever since he'd been asked out by Carter and Eddie. "Weekends are the busiest time at the brewery, though."

"One day on the weekend?" Eddie proposed. "Only until the kids are back in school and summer vacation is over. I can have weekends off again, at least most of them. Plus, I've been thinking. Maybe it's time for me to ask for a transfer."

"You haven't been at Big Bend very long," Carter protested. "Surely they won't move you yet."

"They might, depending on the openings. I'll check."

"I don't want you doing that for me. Er...us," Dare was brave enough to say.

"Same, Eddie. Dare's right. You love your job."

Eddie shrugged. "Carter, it's a job. It doesn't mean as much to me as you. As long as I'm working outside somewhere, I'll be fine. Doesn't have to be at Big Bend. As to the rest, we'll work it all out if we're committed. I suggest going slow and giving us all time to learn what works and what doesn't. And talking. There will probably need to be lots of that. If something's bothering any one of us, letting it fester is foolish."

Carter replied first. "I agree."

Dare was working up his nerve, and he finally found the courage he was seeking. "This is bothering me," he said, touching his cock through his jeans. "I've never been so hard for anyone in my life as I am for you two."

Eddie's smile could have charmed the pants off every man in the vicinity—which just so happened to be Carter and Dare.

"I don't think I can do much of anything at all," Carter said. "Even kissing would hurt. Taking a sudden, deep breath hurts. Maybe I can touch and watch. I'd like to."

Dare's belly quivered. Could he do what he wanted? He believed Eddie and Carter were sincere.

"Also," Eddie said, sitting up so fast the bed bounced. "Mail! Carter, here's yours. Mine's in my pocket."

Carter appeared to be as confused as Dare felt until Eddie passed Carter the envelope. "Oh, awesome."

"What is it?" Dare asked, watching Carter first then Eddie as they pulled out a piece of paper.

"Test results." Eddie dropped his on Dare's chest. "I am a hundred percent clean."

"Same." Carter handed his to Dare.

After looking the results over, Dare set them back on his chest. "I haven't had sex in almost ten years with anything other than my dildos." Dare loved the groans that got him from both men. "And I'm tested for everything annually, at least. I haven't ever had unprotected sex, either—not even with Hank. Guess that says something about the relationship."

"Says that he's gone, and you're ours," Eddie informed him. "Will you trust me and Carter? Let us see you naked? If you're not ready to go without condoms, that's okay. I wasn't planning on having anal sex tonight anyway, just to let you know."

Dare was a little disappointed at that. "No?"

Eddie shook his head. "Not yet. I want to love on you, sure enough."

"I'm good with no condoms," Dare decided. "We're excluding everyone else, just us three."

"We are." Eddie stroked Dare from knee to nipple then took the test results from him. "You don't like pain."

Dare recoiled a little at that. "No, I don't. I had enough of that already."

"I like it," Carter admitted. "Something we should have brought up sooner. I like for Eddie to paddle my ass until I'm begging him to fuck me."

Surprisingly, Dare's cock only got harder. "Really?"

"Really. I like him to be rough with me, but I'm not into doing it to someone else." Carter chuckled. "Go figure."

"And it's not a deal breaker for me. I like slapping Carter's ass, with a paddle, my hand, or even a belt if it's what he wants. I get that need met with him. Don't think I'd want to turn you over my knee."

"I hope not." Dare tugged at his belt buckle. He needed to take his pants and underwear off himself. "I think I'd like watching you and Carter doing that." He got the buckle open then went after the fastening of his jeans. "Please keep talking to me."

"How about I kiss you," Eddie offered.

"I can talk," Carter added. "Doesn't hurt like it did as long as I don't open my mouth too wide, and this way I'm involved more."

"I have to do this part." Dare pulled on the zipper tab.

"You do that. I'm doing this." Eddie bent toward him, mouth open slightly.

Dare parted his lips, eagerly anticipating the kiss.

"You two are so sexy together," Carter said. "Eddie's tan is beautiful against your paler skin. And you, Dare. You have skin that looks so smooth and young. I know it's soft, too. Like warm silk."

Dare listened even as he sank into the kiss. Eddie was definitely in control, except for getting Dare naked. That was all on him. Dare concentrated more on Eddie and Carter, the kiss and the words, so he didn't focus on baring his genitals.

He got the zipper down. Next he toed off his shoes. There was nothing more to do then but lift his hips up and begin shoving his jeans and boxers down. He had to shimmy, and the kiss got sloppier. Carter's voice got huskier the more skin Dare exposed.

Dare couldn't think about his single ball or his thin, curved dick. He wasn't much longer than average there, and he was fine with it. His legs got tangled in the denim and cotton. Dare kicked and wiggled to no avail. He finally had to turn his head enough to ask for help. "Please, Eddie. I can't get them off."

"I'll do it." Eddie kissed him again then moved to sit at Dare's feet. "You have a beautiful dick, and there's nothing unattractive about your ball. It's fat and I love that."

"Are you going to put it in your mouth?" Carter asked. "Suck on it like you do mine? God, that feels so fucking good."

Dare was quickly being reduced to a man who could only whimper. He knew how odd it was to see his single nut, but Carter and Eddie were helping him believe it didn't matter. And maybe, to them, it didn't. Dare could learn to let his self-consciousness go.

Eddie peeled his clothes off, all but Dare's shirt. "Take that off, Dare. Let me see you naked. Show Carter how hot you are."

"Scrawny," Dare argued.

"I won't swat you for that like I would Carter. I will tell you, you are one fine, sexy, son of a bitch. You're thin, sure, but you got definition in your arms and pecs. Your stomach's got a bit of a six pack. There's muscles on you, and you're perfect just like you are."

"I—Eddie!" Dare yelled when Eddie went right down on him, sucking Dare's cock in to the base. "I can't I can't I can't," he gibbered. "Too long. I'll come!"

"Then come," Carter urged. "Forget the shirt and just feel that wet, warm mouth sucking you in. He's got this way of swallowing that's more like a moist fist gripping your dick and jacking you off than you won't believe until you feel it."

Dare felt it all right, and he might have shot his load then had Eddie not palmed his ball. The fear and embarrassment returned.

"No, don't do that, Dare. You shouldn't be ashamed. You're so strong. You survived cancer. You built up a successful business. You are incredible and so sexy," Carter said.

The words helped. Dare relaxed enough to enjoy what was happening again. Eddie licked his cock, tracing veins and flicking at his frenulum. Dare had to move, had to thrust. He did, seeking more friction— that wet heat again.

Eddie went down lower and pulled Dare's sac into his mouth.

The pleasure was exquisite. Dare had avoided that area since the surgery. He'd given up on it ever being an erotic spot.

But oh, it is. It so is.

Eddie rolled his nut around, massaging it with a slick tongue.

Carter kept up the dirty talk, sharing his experiences with Eddie's talented mouth.

Dare started to reach for his dick to jack off, but Carter stopped him with a, "Wait. Don't you want him to suck you again?"

Dare did. He really, really did. He put his hand on his stomach instead and began tracing patterns on it.

Carter joined him, sliding his hand under Dare's shirt to touch skin.

And Eddie let go of his sac. He licked lower, until he could tease Dare's asshole.

Dare was going to die if he didn't get to come soon. Hank hadn't been one for rimming and even a few swipes from Eddie over his pucker was enough to break his resolve not to jerk off.

Eddie pushed his tongue in slightly, then before Dare had his dick in hand, Eddie was back up on it swallowing him down hard and deep. He palmed Dare's ball again, and at the same time, he swallowed.

Dare's shout left his throat aching as cum spurted from his shaft. He was blind with the ecstasy, rutting, thrusting, coming until he was weak and on the verge of falling asleep.

Eddie released Dare's cock, kissing the very tip. Dare was too exhausted to even whimper.

Until Eddie said he was going to get off, too.

Dare pried open one eye just in time to see Eddie get up. He took off his pants—no underwear for him— then got back on the bed. He stared at Dare as he moved to lie on top of him, keeping the weight of his upper body light by planting his elbows above Dare's shoulders.

"This okay?" Eddie wanted to know. He lowered his hips. His thick, long cock was pressed alongside Dare's softening one.

Dare nodded, unable to get his mouth to function.

Then Eddie kissed him, and began to rut, driving his hard length against Dare.

There was little to no chance of Dare getting hard again for a while. He was, after all, close to forty,

But it felt damned good to have such a strong, virile man rubbing off on him, kissing him like Dare mattered.

Dare got his arms up. He started running his hands down Eddie's back. His hand brushed against another—Carter was touching Eddie too. Eddie sped up his thrusts, grunting like an animal with every one of them.

He was magnificent, even when he stopped kissing Dare to instead nibble at his jaw.

"So fucking hot," Carter said, for what might have been the tenth time. Dare wasn't really keeping track.

Eddie widened his legs, bracing them on either side of Dare. He was a powerful beast, driving Dare into the mattress. Dare could imagine being fucked like that, hard and raw and needful. Like he wasn't a skinny older guy who might break.

Eddie wasn't handling him delicately. He put more weight on Dare and frotted like he had to do it or die.

When he came, Eddie buried his face against Dare's neck and sucked. Dare didn't care if he left a mark. He found himself hoping that Eddie would. He hung on while Eddie shook and spilled his cum between them.

"God, my dick tried so hard to get up," Carter said later. "I may start watching even when I'm not injured. Sometimes, at least. Maybe."

Dare tried to think of something witty. He failed, which was okay. Instead he ended up snuggled between Carter and Eddie. It should have felt strange. Hank had never been a cuddler. Dare certainly had never been in the position he was then. Carter wasn't as close to him, but he did have a hand on Dare's chest. Dare made a note not to move around a lot. He didn't want to risk hurting Carter.

He still had questions, doubts, worries. They couldn't compete with the comfort Dare drew from Carter and Eddie. Dare closed his eyes and let everything go but the knowledge he was wanted.

Chapter Twelve

"I have to leave," Dare was whispering to Eddie.

Carter opened one eye and saw them huddled side by side on the edge of the bed. They'd had a good day together yesterday, napping and talking after Eddie and Dare had both came. Carter wished he'd been able to do more than just touch. Still, even that had been enjoyable for him.

Dare was explaining that he had to be at the brewery for a delivery in an hour. "I need to go home and shower. Clean clothes would be great, too. I honestly hadn't expected to spend the night."

"You thought we wouldn't want you because you have one nut?" Eddie asked. "You know better now."

"Your mind can turn on you, Eddie. That's the only way I can think to explain it. The things we can believe about ourselves are probably much worse than what other people could come up with." Dare stood up. He arched his back, stretching.

Carter thought he moved smoothly, sinuously. He definitely approved. Damn it all for him having been attacked. It limited him in so many ways, and Dare was right. Carter's mind was fucking him over with worst-case scenarios and fear. It wasn't getting better, even though his body was healing.

How many times had he awoken during the night, his heart racing and sweat covering him? He kept seeing the moment his attacker came out from behind the door. Carter had hesitated. He'd been stunned. If he'd moved faster, fought harder—

"Oh, I hope we didn't wake you."

Dare's words pulled Carter out of the depressing morass of his thoughts. "No, you two didn't wake me." Carter scooted up carefully until his back was against the headboard. "You could give me a goodbye kiss right here." He tapped his cheek. He longed for a real kiss. *Just as soon as my lips are healed enough.*

"You're coming back when you get done?" Carter hoped he didn't sound as whiny to them as he did to himself.

Dare crawled across the bed. He kissed Carter's cheek. "Yes, I'll come back. Do you want me to bring you anything?"

Carter's stomach chose that moment to rumble.

Eddie laughed. "I think I need to get us some breakfast. You sure you can't join us?"

Dare's remorseful expression made Carter want to hug him. But Dare got up and Carter only realized then that he was dressed.

"I really can't. There's no one else I trust to do this except Mom and she has a doctor's appointment." Dare scrubbed a hand over his face. "Man, I'm going to have to tell her."

"About us?" Carter waited until Dare nodded before going on. "I don't mind if you tell her you're only dating one of us, if it would make it easier. Eddie?"

"I'm going to have to tell my family at some point too, but yeah, we can figure that out later. We don't have to solve everything right now."

"Right," Dare agreed. "I'll need to consider the best way to approach Mom. She wasn't accepting of me until I got sick and Hank left me." Dare gulped. It seemed very loud in the room when he did so. "She might not be able to handle me actually having one boyfriend, much less two. I mean, she *says* she's fine with me being gay, but it's only been more of a theory to her since we made up. Oh, I'm not making any sense."

"Sure you are. Your mom might surprise you, though. Let's hope she does, anyway." Eddie walked with Dare to the door. "See you later."

Carter watched them kiss, just a brush on the cheek. Dare left and Eddie locked the door.

"You ready for some room service?" Eddie came over and plucked a binder off the nightstand. "Here's what they've got."

"What do you say we cuddle on the bed and watch bad movies all day?" Eddie began stacking the pillows up, taking some from the couch to add to the pile.

"Sounds good. I have to get up." Carter was relieved when Eddie merely watched him closely rather than hovering over him. Carter got his feet on the floor then stood. His ribs were definitely the worst cause of pain. He shuffled over to the counter to get a pain pill.

"Here's your water." Eddie set a bottle down for him. "We forgot to ask Dare if he was braver than me with clippers."

Carter took his medicine, washing it down with about half the bottle of water. He'd forgotten about the ugly bald spot until then, but didn't begrudge Eddie for bringing it up. "We can ask him later, or you can just do it. I'd do it myself but raising my arms over my head? Nope. Not wise."

Eddie cupped his face and ran his thumbs along Carter's cheekbones. "You're going to be sexy as hell, you know. Hair, no hair—it doesn't matter. You're always going to be you."

"Smooth talker." Carter appreciated it. "You're going to make sure I don't become a recluse, aren't you?"

"I think you'll make sure of that yourself. I was thinking maybe you could come back to Big Bend with me until you have to return to your job. Dare could maybe even pry himself away from the microbrewery. Show him a bit of our world."

"I'm hardly up for hiking," Carter said wryly. "Walking is enough of a challenge. It'd be nice to get away, though. I feel like I'm going to be jumping at every little thing here."

"You need to be alert. I wish I could stay here and watch over you—"

"I'm an adult," Carter snapped. "Sorry. I don't mean to be a dick."

"I was going to say, but you'd kill me if I tried." Eddie let go of him and leaned against the counter. "Doesn't mean that protective instinct isn't there."

"Right. I'm sorry. Just, I hate being so weak, and I heard Dare. He's right. I think my mind is more damaged than my body."

"There's counseling that might help," Eddie suggested.

"I might go that route if things don't get better. Right now, I think I just need time. And I need to call into work. I vaguely remember you telling me you called and told them I'd been hurt."

"Yeah, I talked to Becca. I told her what happened, figured she'd need all the info so you could be given the time off of work."

"Thanks for that. I want to check in since there were two accounts with deadlines for tomorrow." Then Carter remembered that he no longer had a cell phone. "Shit."

Eddie held out his cell. "Use mine. After you call Becca, you should call your phone carrier. They'll probably overnight you a new phone."

"Let's hope I had at least a partial upgrade. Even with the insurance, there's a deductible." Carter took Eddie's phone. By the time he'd finished the calls, room service had delivered breakfast. Carter ate with as voracious an appetite as his split lips would allow.

"Shower, then movies?" Eddie suggested afterward.

"Sure."

The shower was possibly the best one Carter had ever had. It was funny what a few days of sponge baths could make a person appreciate. Eddie touched him all over, too, washing Carter with a tenderness that Carter reciprocated when it was his turn. He couldn't wash Eddie's hair, due to the sore ribs, but that was okay. He and Eddie were content.

Carter did manage a slow, soapy hand job for Eddie. His own cock wasn't up to playing yet. Carter told himself not to fret over it.

"You're hurting. It's not the fun kind of pain, either, so give yourself a break." Eddie turned off the shower. "Come on. I'll dry you off."

* * * *

During the second movie, Eddie's cell phone rang. He paused the TV then checked his phone. "Detective

Dennis. Maybe." Eddie answered while Carter tried not to tense up.

Clenching his muscles made everything hurt. It was better to relax.

"Yes, Carter is here. Hang on." Eddie handed the phone over to him.

Carter took it. He was leery of talking to the police Detective because he feared bad news. *Man up already.* "This is Carter."

"Mr. Hausemann, your neighbor called in a report about a prowler. She saw him leaving your apartment."

Carter gasped, locking gazes with Eddie. "Did...? Was he arrested?"

Eddie's eyes widened and he mouthed, "Mark?"

"Unfortunately, no. She said he was leaving and by the time she called it in, he was gone. We went over and checked it out. There's a lot of damage inside. I know you were just released yesterday, but it'd be helpful if you could meet my partner and I there. We don't know what, if anything, was stolen."

Carter didn't want to go. It was too soon.

But Eddie looked at him as if Carter was strong and he could do this frightening thing that was being asked of him.

"If you could give me a time, see if it works with what we've got to handle already, that'd be great."

Carter took a deep, calming breath. "We can head over there now." If he put it off, he might back out completely.

"That'd be good. We'll see you in about thirty minutes then." Detective Dennis hung up.

Carter was still holding the phone to his ear when Eddie took it from him. "Someone broke into the apartment." Carter was turning numb, the pain from his injuries ceasing to exist over the complete nothingness filling him. "He broke in, and it sounds like a mess and I didn't want to go back yet but—" He had to.

"I'll be right there with you," Eddie promised. "I'll hold your hand, if that's what you need. Fuck what anyone else says."

"Thank you." Carter closed his eyes. "I can't feel my body. I'm not sure that's bad."

"It's too much shock, all this happening." Eddie sat began rubbing Carter's hands, as if he were chasing away a chill. "Anyone would be disturbed. The thing is, maybe he fucked up. Maybe there's something left in your apartment that can help the cops nail his ass to the wall."

"I think they police have already been in there since they need me to tell them if anything's been stolen." Carter shivered then, the numbness fleeing and leaving him cold and tired. "I wanted more time before I had to go back. I don't have it. That's all there is to this. It's just stupid to be so scared. I'm not the only person who's ever been attacked in their own home, but I'm probably the biggest wuss over it."

Eddie was growling before Carter finished speaking. "Nothing you feel is stupid, honey. Don't even start that. You don't know how other people react, either. Doesn't matter what they do anyway. We're talking about you, not some nameless person who was victimized."

"I fucking hate that word. I don't want to be a victim." Carter pulled his hands free so he could get up. "I read somewhere it doesn't matter. You can be strong or weak in response to a crime. You're still a victim."

Eddie got up when Carter did. Carter watched the confident way Eddie held himself as he walked over to get his keys and wallet. Those broad shoulders would never be weighed down by self-doubt.

"What you've got to remember is, you're more than a one word description, Carter. You're a combination of many, many things. Words, experiences, thoughts—everything you've ever lived through. That's what you are—not just one singular word."

Carter ducked his head. "You're right. Thanks, Eddie."

"Anytime. Let me get your flip-flops and a shirt. Those sweats you have on will be fine." Eddie helped Carter get dressed before putting on a shirt and tennis shoes. "All right, let's do this."

"Can I use your phone?" Carter asked.

"Sure. Going to text Dare?" Eddie gave his phone back to Carter.

Carter ran his thumb over the screen. "Yeah. I don't want him feeling left out of the loop, and maybe between you and him, I won't flip out."

"You can do this." Eddie kissed his brow. "I have faith in you."

They left the hotel and were at the apartment complex less than twenty minutes later. Carter's heart bounced around in his chest like a bunny trying to escape from a wolf. He understood exactly what a swoon was because he was close to doing one.

"I'm right here," Eddie murmured. "The police are here too, and there's Jerri peeking out her curtains being nosy. Thank God she is."

Eddie kept up the chatter. It soothed Carter's nerves. He was determined to do this thing, to walk into the apartment and not fall apart. Eddie could see him weak and doubtful, so could Dare, but to let strangers see him that way was too much for Carter.

By the time they reached his door where the Detectives were waiting, Carter had himself under control. Or, he was hopeful, at least it seemed that way outwardly. Inside he was a jittery mess.

"Mr. Hausemann, Mr. Canales." Detective Dennis nodded to them both.

Carter caught a speculative gleam in the man's eye but shrugged it off. He wasn't going to dwell on someone else's issues.

"There you two are," Jerri said, coming out of her apartment. "Oh, Carter. How are you?"

If she couldn't tell by all the bruising, he wasn't going to point out that he felt like hell. "Good, Jerri. How are you?"

"Oh fine, fine," she said, waving him off. "I'm glad to see your boyfriend is here. Eddie is such a nice young man."

Dennis coughed and Carter glanced at him. "Problem?"

The detective hadn't asked about Carter's sexuality. Then again, since Carter had told him about running into Mark at The Circle, he supposed there'd been no need. Not many straight guys would hang out at a gay bar. In fact, none of them would.

It just annoyed him that no one would have asked him if he was straight, nor would he have thrown that out there if he was. Detective Dennis had asked what kind of relationship Carter had with Mark, and that answer had been simple — none. Now he expected Dennis to ask him other more personal questions.

"If you could come inside please," Detective Janie Flores said.

Detective Dennis smiled slightly at Jerri. "You'll have to let us have these two for a little while. Then you can catch up." He nodded toward Carter and Eddie. "I'm assuming Mr. Canales is going in with you?"

Carter nodded. Hadn't Eddie told him the nurse, Cindy, said Dennis was a bigot? He seemed to be holding it in if that was true.

Carter forgot about the issue when he entered the apartment. "Jesus."

"Bastard," Eddie rumbled.

The entryway was littered with pieces of foam and paper. They walked through it and stopped in the living area. Carter was stunned by the destruction. He had the absurd thought that he'd never get his deposit back now and almost giggled like a lunatic.

"He—and your neighbor is sure it was a man—really did a number on the place," Detective Flores said. "She also swore that she saw some of the man's hair hanging out the back of the ski mask, like he hadn't pulled the mask down properly in the back."

"Brown?" Carter asked. His furniture was ruined. The stuffing had been torn out of the shredded cushions, his TV had a crack running vertically all the way across it. The framed art was either gone or somewhere in the mess on the floor.

"Yes, brown. That doesn't prove it was the guy you worked with, since there are any number of men in Odessa with brown hair." Flores stepped past Carter. "I understand this is difficult, but if you could take the time to try. The fingerprint dust doesn't help, either, I'm sure, but it was necessary."

"There's so much..." Carter had to stop before his voice started to quaver. He couldn't even see more than a few inches of his floor in the living room. "I don't know if I'll be able to tell what, if anything, is missing."

"Your bedroom might be the best place to figure that out," Detective Dennis said. "If this guy is fixated on you sexually, he might take underwear, other clothes."

Carter's stomach was trying to shove his breakfast back up. He willed himself to keep it together. "This seems more like someone who hates me."

"People are weird," Dennis offered. "Something goes wrong in some of them and they act in the complete opposite of what a normal, rational person would do. This guy is escalating, and he's already proved he's willing to hurt you. Whether his intent then was to knock you unconscious and abduct you or something else, I don't know. And he went after Mr. Canales' via his truck."

"Because I'm Carter's boyfriend," Eddie said, but the way he did it made the words come out more like a grand proclamation than anything else. He wasn't telling Dennis because it was any of the detective's business. He said it because he was proud of it. "That's not going to be a problem here, is it?"

Detective Flores frowned. "We're professionals. Our personal beliefs should never come into our work, whether we're for or against homosexuality. Plus, you know, your boyfriend was hovering over you at the hospital or that other guy from the microbrewery was. We're not stupid or inept, gentlemen."

Detective Dennis let loose an irritated sound. "Eh, it was Cindy. I said some politically incorrect crap when I was a stupid kid and she'll never forget it. People can change. I was a little slower getting there, but it happened."

"I never dated Mark," Carter felt compelled to say then, despite his earlier decision. "I turned him down."

"Yes, you told us. Mr. Hausemann. Why don't you try to calm down a little?" Dennis suggested. "You look like you're about to bolt right out of your skin."

So much for keeping the panic inside.

Eddie took a hold of his hand, which helped. Carter gave him a tiny smile. "Okay. Um, the living room, all the wall art is either gone or destroyed."

"I'm thinking the last one," Flores said. "There are parts of wooden and metal frames over there. Paper and canvas, too."

Carter dared to step farther into the room. He studied the mess on the floor. "Yeah, I think you're right."

He turned and headed for the kitchen since it was on the way to his room. The refrigerator was open, its contents strewn about. Milk, eggs, and other food items congealed into gross puddles. All of the dishes were broken, including his drinking glasses. The pantry was empty, the food in it ruined. "Unless he stole my pans, I don't think anything's gone from here."

The bathroom was in a similar state, his hygiene products dumped out on the floor. "No scary message on the mirror," he whispered.

"This is probably scary enough without one," Dennis said.

Carter had delayed it as long as he could. All that was left was the bedroom.

"I'm right here with you."

Eddie's presence was Carter's anchor, keeping him from floating off into a panic.

He stopped at the bedroom door and gasped. "It's not wrecked like the rest of the place!"

"We're thinking maybe it was his messed up way of apologizing for hurting you here," Flores said. "Or, he could just be bonkers, or he was afraid he'd get caught and didn't have time to ransack this room."

Carter forced his feet to move. Walking through that doorway was one of the hardest things he'd ever done. He couldn't help but dart a nervous glance to the door.

The detectives came in, and as if he knew it was bothering Carter to see it, Dennis leaned on the door, pinning it to the wall. He gave Carter a short nod.

Carter scowled. "I can't remember if the blankets were like that or not. I don't think so. I usually make my bed every morning because it keeps the room from looking messy. Sometimes I forget when I'm in a hurry, and I'd left several days before to visit Eddie."

"I wonder if he was staying here." Eddie muttered. "That seems like something someone this disturbed would do."

"It's possible. He may have done just that, then had some kind of breakdown that set him off on a violent streak," Dennis said. "You can touch whatever you need to.

Carter managed to get closer to the bed. The idea of someone who'd attacked him sleeping there, touching his clothes and personal items was worse than the assault itself. Carter felt violated in a deeper way he couldn't describe.

And he couldn't touch the blankets. "What if he stayed here before, when I was in Big Bend?" Carter was so close to freaking out. He had to hold it together. "He could have."

"We won't know until we catch him, and maybe not even then." Flores gestured to the dresser. "Could you check and see if any of your clothing is gone? Or anything from the box on the top?"

Carter kept his cuff links, keys, and other bits of this and that in a wooden jewelry box that had been his mother's. The relief at seeing the box and knowing he hadn't lost it almost overwhelmed him. She'd had only a few pieces of jewelry, none of it worth much monetarily. The sentimental value was priceless. "It was my mom's." Staring at it, Carter crossed over to the dresser. Fingerprint powder covered the surface and knobs on it. Even the jewelry box had been dusted. Carter's hand shook as he opened the lid. "It's empty. God damn it, everything is gone—her necklaces, her ring. There was a picture." Carter shook his head. He had others in the closet, unless they'd been taken.

"I need to check the closet." He'd come back to the dresser.

Seeing that his mother's things had been stolen infuriated Carter. Inside the closet, he barely noticed whether or not any clothes were missing. What he did note was that the photo album was gone. "He took the pictures!"

From that moment on, Carter knew he was going to get past the fear, because the anger was going to suffocate it. He told the detectives what else was missing—clothes, a book, a pair of shoes. As far as he could tell, that was it.

"I'd suggest a cleaning agency if you can afford it," Detective Dennis said. "We're not supposed to play favorites, but it isn't like I get a commission for telling you O'Harahan's is good at what they do."

"They are," Detective Flores agreed. "Pricey, too, so you'll have to decide whether or not to use them or to have your friends help out instead."

Detective Dennis chuckled. "Friends are great free labor. Most you gotta do is feed them pizza and hand them a beer."

"And that's why I wouldn't help you last time you had to move." Detective Flores stopped joking and turned her attention back to Carter. "I'd recommend not staying here. We found nothing that could help us when we examined Mr. Canales' truck. Whoever is doing this is smart, but maybe he's getting sloppy. We'll know more when we run the prints. Unfortunately, that could take a while."

"If the suspect has a Texas license, his fingerprints should be on file," Detective Dennis added. "Let's hope we get that lucky."

"How long is a while?" Eddie asked.

"Could be a few weeks. It's not as quick or easy as it is on TV."

Carter thanked the detectives for their help after they had all left the apartment. Carter locked the door, for all the good that had done before. He watched the detectives walk to their cars.

Jerri came out to chat. "Those police officers seem know what they're doing?"

"I hope so." He also hoped he could find a way to politely escape. He didn't feel like talking to his neighbor right then.

"You need to talk to the people at the office here," Jerri suggested. "They might let you out of your lease—not that I want to see you gone. If you do leave, my luck some loud and obnoxious Bible thumpers will move in there. I already have some on the other side of me. They don't bother knocking on my door anymore." She cackled. "They scare easy."

"Jerri, I think I need to take Carter back to the hotel. He's still recovering." Eddie cupped Carter's elbow. "You have my number. Thank you for being such a great neighbor."

Jerri flapped a hand at him. "Oh, pshaw! He's a good boy and so are you. I don't have anything else to do but be nosy."

They left after that and to Carter's surprise, Dare met them at the hotel in the parking lot.

"Who knew," Dare said. "I *can* designate after all."

Chapter Thirteen

"For what it's worth, I think taking Carter to Big Bend is probably the safest thing for him."

"I'm right here," Carter told Dare. "And I love going there, but how are you going to feel about it?"

Dare shrugged one shoulder. "Your safety needs to be the priority here. Besides, I talked to Mom about hiring someone to manage the brewery. She asked me why, and I told her I was dating someone." Dare's smile lit up his whole face. "She squealed. She was so happy. I don't know that she'll feel that way when she finds out all of it. It was nice to know she really was past the gay thing."

"Who'd you tell her you were dating?" Eddie asked. "Me or Carter?"

"I didn't give her a name. I told her I was keeping it to myself for a while. I thought she was going to brain me."

"My mom would have done so to me. She'd have sicced the sibs on me, too, and I'd have been babbling all in no time." Eddie's expression wavered between cautious and hopeful. "That reminds me. I bet some of my family would come help—"

"No, no, no, no, no," Carter said, shaking his head and actually moving a few inches further from Eddie. "No way. This is not how I want to meet your family. I'll crack into my savings and hire the company recommended to us."

Eddie was kind of relieved. He wasn't eager to have his life dissected by his family. He'd have put up with it to help Carter.

"I was also thinking," Dare began. "I wouldn't mind trying what Eddie suggested. If you two want to mess around some and let me participate via Skype or FaceTime, whatever, that might really be hot."

Carter grimaced. "I don't know if I can do anything until my ribs get better. Well, I can give a hand job."

Dare's eyebrows went up and he shifted in his seat, not so subtly adjusting his dick. "Oh? Do tell."

"We agreed that was okay, right?" Carter asked.

"We did," both Dare and Eddie confirmed.

Eddie wouldn't have done it otherwise, and Carter wouldn't have either. "We were showering this morning. I can't be around Carter or you without getting a hard on." He liked the way that made Dare blush. "Carter got the conditioner out and put a good amount in his hand. God, Dare. He knows how to jack a man off. You should let him show you."

"I should?" Dare squeaked.

"Oh, I could do that while Eddie fucks you," Carter proposed.

Eddie liked Carter's idea a whole lot.

Dare was now touching his dick through his pants. "He c-could."

That was agreement enough for Eddie. He stood then pulled Dare up from his seat on the couch. Carter was on the bed, watching them. "I can." Eddie kissed Dare, licking between his parted lips. Dare tasted like hops, just faintly. Eddie didn't know if that was his imagination or not, but either way, he liked it.

Dare moaned and wrapped his arms around Eddie's neck. Eddie held Dare by the nape and plundered his mouth until he was sure Dare's lips were swollen. He nibbled the bottom one, then steered Dare over to the bed. "You want to get naked for us, sweet stuff? I'm going to get the lube and—you sure about the condoms?"

Dare swallowed, his prominent Adam's apple bobbing twice. "I'm sure we can go without. I brought my results, too—"

Eddie let Carter deal with that. He believed Dare, and Carter probably did too. Eddie got the lube from his bag and a few bottles of water he'd stashed in the mini-fridge. He set the water down and watched Dare remove his clothes.

Carter praised everything about Dare, from his lightly sculpted shoulders to his long toes.

"Monkey toes," Dare scoffed. "I can pinch a man's junk off with them."

"I'll keep that in mind," Carter retorted. "And we'll just have to make sure you're a happy man, won't we?"

Dare wasn't as nervous as he had been yesterday, Eddie was proud to note. His hands still trembled on occasion, but he was smiling and joking more.

Eddie bent to place soft kisses on the parts of Carter's uninjured face. It kind of stopped the conversation. No one seemed to mind.

Then he straightened up. He waited until both men were watching him before taking his clothes off. Eddie knew he was well-built. Part of it was good genes and part was living a healthy lifestyle. He had a nice fat dick that was a gift—at least he thought so. At any rate, he appreciated having it.

Eddie cupped his heavy nuts with one hand while tugging on his left nipple ring with the other. Dare's eyes widened.

"I—how did I not see that yesterday? That's so—ungh." Dare fisted his own length. "Carter had his pierced, too?"

"The night we took the tour," Carter filled in. "You should get yours done when I get back. I think mine have closed up already."

"You didn't see mine yesterday because we were busy at first, then we were asleep. When you woke up, I'd put my shirt on so I could open the door for room service and not have 'em drool." Eddie laughed along with his men over that, then he locked his gaze on Dare's. Eddie waved his cock at him. "So tell me. You want this hard and deep, fast, slow? You tell me. I don't care, just as long as you get off on it."

A fine sheen of sweat broke out on Dare's brow. "I—no one ever asked me before. I think, maybe slow at first? Then…if I can take it—"

"Oh you can, sweet stuff. You can take all of this."

Carter leaned over enough to run his fingertip over Eddie's slit. "You can, and you'll love it. Have you ever had a dick this size in you before?"

There went that Adam's apple again. Eddie was getting a strong urge to suck in it and mark Dare just a little.

"I haven't. Hank was maybe average and before him? Well, just no. I have a dildo close to that size."

Now it was Eddie's turn to moan. "Damn, Dare. You're going to have to bring some of them over next time and let us fuck you with them."

"God, yes," Carter agreed. "I can do that, push a thick dildo into your ass and make you scream."

"I'm not far from it now," Dare huffed.

Eddie grinned. Both of his men just made him happy. "Get in bed, Dare. I want you to straddle Carter's hips so he can reach your dick. Put your hands on the headboard, 'cause I'm gonna make sure you beg me to fuck you hard."

Dare wasted no time doing as he was told. Eddie poured some lube onto Carter's hand. He'd put some on his in a bit so he could finger Dare open, but first...

"Again? Oh God!" Dare exclaimed when Eddie pushed his ass cheeks apart. "I didn't expect—"

Eddie shut him up with a lick right over his pucker. He was aware of Carter playing with Dare's ball and was glad they'd found something they could do together. It'd be even better when Carter was able to get hard again. Eddie didn't think it'd take as long as Carter expected it to, not with Dare joining them.

Dare made plenty of whimpering noises, and he started pleading at the same moment Eddie shoved his tongue into Dare's tight hole. Eddie growled over the sensitive skin, and scraped his teeth over it too, though he was careful not to get too rough. When Dare's ring was glistening with spit, Eddie pulled back and got the lube.

"Please hurry," Dare begged. "Please, Eddie, Carter, I want more."

"You're getting it," Eddie told him right before pushing two wet fingers into his ass.

Dare mewled like an overgrown kitten, and arched his back like one wanting to be petted. Eddie did that, from the inside out, loosening Dare's ass up and playing with his gland.

"His dick is dripping, Eddie. You should see it."

"Bet it's pretty. Describe it in great detail to me."

Dare made another breathy, wordless sound. He seemed to really like the dirty talk. Hearing it, at least.

"There's this one vein right here—" Carter did something that pulled a long, drawn-out moan from Dare. "I can't wait to lick it. It runs right up to the underside of his head. His whole dick is a pretty pink, the tip's darker, and that little slit of his is spitting out pre-cum like you wouldn't believe."

Eddie fitted a third finger into Dare's pucker. He longed to slide into the gripping heat of Dare's ass, to ride him bare and come in him. Eddie wanted to fuck both of his men and use a plug to keep it in them. Seemed like a good idea to share. "We're going to get some butt plugs, and I'll be plugging both of you up so you have my spunk in you. Dare, imagine carrying around mine and Carter's cum in you. We'd each fuck you then send you off to work with a fat plug. Every time you took a step or sat down, you'd be reminded of us."

Dare wasn't the only one who moaned then. Carter was every bit as eager for it as they were.

Eddie turned his fingers and curled them over Dare's gland. "I could just do this until you come. Would you like that?"

"F-fuck me," Dare stuttered out. He moved his hips and moaned again.

Eddie fingered him a little longer until his own dick ached and he had to be inside Dare. "You're ready for me."

"Was ready minutes ago," Dare complained.

Eddie grinned and got up behind Dare. He rubbed his dick up and down Dare's crease, teasing him. "Oh yeah? I think you need a little more time."

"Please. I'm begging. You said I'd beg and... Eddie!"

Eddie had thrust, sinking his crown into the tight vise of Dare's ass. He hooked his arms under Dare, crossing them over his chest. "Fuck, you are something else." Eddie steadily pushed his cock in, until his balls were pressed to Dare's. "Jesus, Carter, you're going to love fucking him."

Eddie could feel the jostling from Carter jacking Dare off, and the internal rippling of those soft anal walls clenching around his dick. It was maddeningly erotic, a more intense threesome than Eddie had ever participated in before because they were all in it for the long haul.

The lack of condom was making it hard to keep from rutting away like a mindless beast. Just the idea of it alone—the trust, the commitment—was enough to test Eddie's resolve to move at Dare's pace.

When Dare wiggled his butt and his inner grip loosened a little, Eddie started moving, taking long strokes in and out. He paused every time he was in to the hilt, just to revel in the experience.

After several minutes, Dare mewled and began shoving back against him.

"He's close," Eddie heard Carter say.

Well, Eddie was too. He tightened his hold on Dare and began to thrust with more force and speed. His balls bounced against Dare's sac, his hips pounded Dare's ass. Dare's inner muscles massaged and milked Eddie's cock so perfectly and he didn't think he'd be able to last much longer.

Then Dare keened and Eddie's dick was held so perfectly in that velvet grip, he was toast. Eddie could only hang on and shudder while he came. His climax seemed endless, so powerful he was sure every cell in his body was flooded with pleasure.

When he was able to think, he slowly released Dare, whose arms shook. He was still bracing himself on the headboard, and Eddie was all but lying on him. "Sorry. You kinda did me in, sweet stuff."

Dare grunted, as if he couldn't talk yet.

Eddie was a little smug about that. He carefully withdrew his cock from Dare's ass, watching the cum dribble out. On impulse, he licked at a little of it. Dare yelped and Carter asked what happened.

"He—he licked my asshole!" Dare said.

"Oh, man, I bet that was something," Carter replied. "Eddie's a kinky guy, which I happen to love about him. Have you ever heard of snowballing?"

"I'm not naïve," Dare told him. "I just didn't know people did it outside of porn."

Eddie licked him again just to reassure him that yes, people did. He patted Dare's butt when he made another startled sound. "You'll be as dirty as we are in no time at all, Dare."

"I'll take your word for it." Dare rolled off to plop beside Carter. "Oh! I got—you have cum on your face and—"

"Maybe you can lick him clean," Eddie suggested. He would have done it had he not been tonguing Dare's ass a minute ago.

"I can?"

Carter closed his eyes. "You so can."

It was an amazing sight to watch Dare tenderly lick the spunk off Carter. Eddie noted too that Carter's cock got half hard. Eddie cupped it through his sweats, just wanting to feel Carter's burgeoning desire.

"I can't get all the way," Carter complained.

"Between your pain meds and being hurt, that's no surprise," Dare told him. "I didn't have an erection for a long time after I was diagnosed and treated. A long time."

"Well, you're cock is working fine now, and you taste good, man." Carter's lips curled up on the side that wasn't split. "Got some right here." He licked a spot on them. "So I know how you taste now."

Eddie fondled Carter's penis for a little while longer, then he got up to use the bathroom. He brushed his teeth, too, because he *would* be kissing Dare and Carter again in a few minutes. Carter, gently, and maybe not on the mouth, but still.

When he came out of the bathroom, Carter and Dare were perusing the room service menu.

"We should just order pizza," Carter suggested. "It's cheaper, and I could go for hot, greasy food right now."

"Sounds good to me. Dare?" Eddie asked.

"I'm in. I don't think I can move to get up and I need to pee. I'm in trouble, guys."

Eddie laughed along with Carter. "Come on, lazy bones, I'll help you.

The delightful shriek he got for pulling Dare up and right onto his shoulder in a fireman's carry was priceless.

"What are you doing?" Dare demanded.

Eddie cupped one lean butt cheek and gave it a squeeze. "Wouldn't want you to lie in bed and suffer, so I'm taking you to the bathroom. Need me to hold it and aim for you?"

"I should say yes," Dare huffed.

Then he surprised Eddie by pushing a finger into Eddie's crack. "What're you doing back there?"

"Playing?" Dare asked. "Do you not like any touching there?"

"To my asshole?" Eddie didn't wait for an answer. "I don't mind a finger or two on occasion while I'm getting sucked or I'm fucking someone. Getting rimmed is fine with me almost any time. I don't bottom."

"I can—" Dare scrambled to hang onto him when Eddie settled him on his feet. "Carter and I could rim you and you'd be fine with that?"

Eddie's shaft should not have been trying to firm up already. "More than fine with it." He patted Dare's backside. "I'll leave you to it."

Dare was gawking at him when Eddie left the bathroom.

Carter was gawking at him too. Eddie winked at Carter. "What?"

"Well now I have this vision of me and Dare taking turns licking your hole until you come."

Eddie hated to dispel Carter's fantasy, but keeping expectations real was important. "I have never come from being rimmed. It feels good. Don't get me wrong. Just not as good as a wet mouth or a tight ass around my dick."

Carter glanced at said body part. "How was it? To fuck without a condom?"

"Magnificent," Dare hollered, not quite too loudly.

"What he said." Eddie plopped down by Carter. "You can feel more. I think it's up here that makes the biggest difference, though." He tapped his temple. "And I would never have done it if I didn't..." He rolled his lips in. He wasn't in love with Dare yet, was he? Eddie honestly didn't know.

"We're a good fit, the three of us." Carter sounded as happy as possible, considering his injuries. "Thank you for letting me be me."

Eddie kissed the tip of Carter's nose. "Same goes, honey. Now, how about those pizzas?"

Chapter Fourteen

Dare walked into his brewery and knew almost immediately he was about to be grilled. His mother stood by her desk, her arms crossed over her chest. She had the same expression on her face she'd get when Dare got in trouble at school. The difference now was that he was an adult and had been for a long time. That still didn't curb his inner cringe or the urge to start apologizing. He didn't.

"I went by your house last night to bring you some of my chicken casserole, but you weren't home."

Well, at least he knew where this was going.

"Mom, I told you I'm seeing someone."

Dee tilted her head down and yet managed to stare up at him at the same time. "Yes, but you weren't home this morning, either. I don't know who you're seeing. You haven't seen fit to share that with me. Don't you think it's moving fast, though?"

Dare yearned to get a cup of coffee. He needed caffeine to be able to deal with this inquisition. "No, I don't. If you'll recall, there were several days I've taken off for a few hours this past week. Where do you think I was then? I was with—" *That look. Oh God, how do moms do that?* "Carter," he finished, yet that didn't sit right with him. Dee would be angrier at him if he lied now and she found out the truth, via him or otherwise, later on. Dare heaved a great sigh. "Mom, can I get a cup of coffee then we can have this conversation?"

"I guess," she sniffed. "I don't have a problem with who you date, now, but I do think sex isn't something to be taken lightly."

"Oh believe me, we're not taking it lightly at all," Dare muttered.

"I heard that!"

"Do you want coffee?" Dare headed for the tasting area, where there would be a fresh pot waiting on him. He hoped.

"Yes, thank you. Two sugars."

Like he didn't know how his mom took it. She always told him anyway just like she always asked if he wanted onions when she ought to know by now that he hated them. Those kinds of quirks made him love his mom even more. The thought of losing her scared the crap out of him, but he was going to choose to be honest with her and hope she would come around to accept the relationship, if not immediately, then in the near future.

Dare got their coffees and greeted his employees along the way. When he handed his mom her cup, he asked her to come into his office so they could speak privately.

Dee sat down and folded her hands in her lap. She appeared to be poised so properly, and Dare knew it was her way of dealing with being afraid. Was she afraid for him? He kind of thought so.

"Okay, Mom. Here's the thing. I love you. I will always love you. I loved you when you didn't talk to me after I came out. I loved you for changing your ways and beliefs. I loved you for helping me when Hank ran off. I love that you encouraged me to build this," he waved at the general area, "And that you had faith in me to do it. I love you, period."

"I—"

"Please, let me get this all out before it dissipates in my head and I lose it." Dare waited until she closed her mouth. "Okay, so I realized something. Part of why I haven't had a relationship is because I was afraid you would cut me off again. Me being gay...that's one thing, I guess. You said you accepted it, but that was after I was alone. What would happen if I dated a guy? Would seeing us together bring back that part of you that disowned me?" Tears pricked his eyes but he blinked them away. "And I felt like a freak, too. Scrawny, with, you know, just the one. But Mom," he leaned forward, elbows and forearms on his desk. "I don't want to live my life alone. I mean—like I said—I love you. It's not enough. I thought this place would be enough, too, but it isn't. I'd give this brewery up for someone of my own, if I had to."

"Dare, I..." Dee wiped at tears on her cheeks. "I know I hurt you. I did something no parent ever should do. I'll always be sorry for it. I wish I'd known I was part of the reason you weren't dating. I want you to be happy. I believe that means loving someone in a...a physical way. I loved your dad something fierce, and when he died, I wanted to die, too."

Dare remembered that time. It'd been horrible to wake up and have his dad tell him goodbye, then to find out his dad had been killed by a drunk driver on the way to work. Dare had been eleven, and he'd learned that life could change and even be gone in an instant then.

"I couldn't, of course," Dee said. "I had you. Then I didn't, because I was a fool. I wish I would have told you it was okay, that I wanted you to find someone special. Someone you'd give up everything for. You've been working yourself to a nub for years. I'm proud of you, but you deserve more. And that's what I want for you. Someone who deserves you, not just someone to have sex with."

That was as uncomfortable for her to say as it was for him to hear. However, they were both adults. Dare shouldn't want to plug his ears when his mother mentioned him and sex.

"Can you tell me that's what you've found? Someone who appreciates you?" she asked.

Dare figured it was now or never. They were baring their hearts already. "I can't say I'm in love, or vice versa, but I do see this heading there. As for the sex, Mom. We're healthy adults who are attracted to each other. We also respect each other and trust each other, and we all want the same thing. A long abiding relationship," *God help me,* "for the three of us."

Dee was silent for so long Dare started to sweat despite the cool temperature of his office. He was a jerk for upsetting her. He should have waited. Finally he couldn't stand it anymore. "Mom? Are you — do you hate me now?"

Dee's bottom lip started to quiver. "That you can even ask me such a question when you're doing this to hurt me —"

"Whoa." That stopped Dare from feeling guilty right there. "No. That's just wrong. This has *nothing* to do with you and everything to do with two men who make me feel like I'm special to them. And you know what? We talk. We confront our problems. We're not stupid, and we know people aren't accepting of non-traditional relationships. We know and we're still going to make it work. Why? Because we want it to. Because we don't think there's a limit on our hearts' capacity for love. You have no idea what's been happening."

"How could I?" Dee asked, sobbing afterward. "How, when you kept all this inside? Then you... You just spring this on me! It's—"

"Unnatural?" Dare said, keeping his voice soft. "Against the will of God? Wrong in the eyes of society?" All things she had told him when he'd come out to her.

Dee snatched a tissue out of the box on his desk. She dabbed at her eyes, then blew her nose. The tip was red, a sign of more tears to come. Dare had seen her cry often enough to know this.

"I said those things. I won't hurt you that way again, but I don't know if I can accept this."

It was like being nineteen and rejected all over again. Dare stood up so fast his chair toppled over backward. "You don't have to. I do. And I have." He left his office before he ended up saying something he'd never be able to take back. He of all people knew how sharply and deep words could cut.

He couldn't help but wonder how Eddie's family would react. Hopefully better than Dee had.

* * * *

"I'm not going to be getting out of here until after midnight at the earliest," Dare explained to Eddie and Carter, who had him on speakerphone. "I didn't want to presume and just come over then."

"Dare, you're always welcome. You're a part of us, right?" Eddie said. "We want you with us as much as possible."

"But I'll be worn out." He already was. "I don't think I'll be up to anything."

"You don't have to be. Just…come sleep with us. Let us hold you. That's all. It isn't all about sex. It's about the connection between us."

"Eddie's right," Carter added. "We're still building the relationship between us. I just want as much time with you both as I can have. I really wish you could come with us to Big Bend."

Dare wanted to. Right then, he wanted to be with Carter and Eddie more than anything. The tension between him and his mother was keeping him on edge, but he had another private tour that evening. Dare hadn't yet told his boyfriends about his conversation with Dee. He'd prefer to do so in person, so he'd wait.

"I'll see if I can take off at least one full day." God, that didn't sound like much at all. If Dee wasn't upset with him, he could ask her to run the place. She knew how as well as he did. Maybe it was time for him to seriously start hiring for management employees. He could afford to pay someone a decent wage so he could have more time off.

"Whatever you can manage."

"I'd best go. I'll see you both later. Be safe." Dare disconnected the call after Carter and Eddie said their goodbyes. He tucked his phone away and turned around to find his mother watching him. Dare waited for her to say something and when she didn't, he went back to counting the inventory they'd gotten in.

The next time he checked, Dee wasn't there.

Somehow, he needed to find the time to write up a good help wanted ad. That would entail figuring out just what he wanted in a person who would be able to run Dare's while he was away. *Or I could sell it.* He'd had plenty of offers on the place. Now that he had something — someone, two men to be specific — he could potentially love, selling might be an option further down the road. Dare wouldn't make any rash decisions, but he did concede it was time to start thinking about the future in more terms than quarterly reports.

He was checking the barrels when Archie approached him. Archie was a great employee with a very sensitive palate. Dare stopped what he was doing when Archie called out to him. "Yeah, what's up?"

Archie glanced over his shoulder before answering. He walked over until he was almost in Dare's personal space, which was unlike him. "Have you seen your mom today? She seems like she doesn't feel well and I'm worried about her."

A bolt of alarm went through Dare. "I saw her a couple of hours ago. What do you mean?"

"She was in the break room a few minutes ago and told me she didn't feel good, so she was going home. She's never gone home sick before. I asked her if I should come get you but she told me not to bother you. Like you wouldn't want to know," he scoffed.

"Of course I do. Thank you, Archie." Should he call his mom? Dare disposed of that idea. It seemed cowardly on both of their parts if his mom didn't answer. And, if she really was sick, she might need medical care.

"Archie, can you call and cancel that tour I have in a couple of hours? Offer them a fifty percent discount for the inconvenience."

"I can do that for you, sure. The info on your desk, in that calendar?" Archie asked.

Dare dusted his hands on his pants. "Yes, it should be open right to it. Thanks, Archie. Can you also see to the running of things here?"

Always before, either Dare or his mother was there. Archie lit up like a hundred watt bulb had been turned on inside him. "I can! I mean… I can, Dare. You can trust me."

Archie's enthusiasm was something Dare needed to think about. He might have options to move him and other people who were interested, into more authoritative positions. Right now he needed to go check on Dee.

"Thanks. Call if there's any problems or questions."

"I will," Archie vowed.

Dare left and sent a text to his guys as he walked to his car. *Tour off. Mom is sick. Don't know where I'll be in a few hours. Her place or with y'all.*

When Carter and Eddie both texted back individually, Dare knew Carter had gotten his new cell phone. Both men sent wishes for Dee to feel better. Dare hadn't told them about his discussion with Dee. He wanted to do that in person, not via text or phone.

Dee lived two blocks from him in the same house he'd grown up in. Dare saw her car in the drive and parked his at the curb. He got out and jogged up the sidewalk, saying a silent prayer that Dee wouldn't refuse to let him in. Dare knocked on the door, even though he had a key. If his mom was so mad at him she had to leave work, walking right into her house would be a mistake

But Dee opened the door. Her skin had a grayish cast to it and she was sweating. Granted, they were in West Texas, and it was hot, but Dare could feel the cool air flowing out through the screen door. It wasn't hot in the house.

"Dare. I'm sorry. I don't feel well."

Dare put his hand on the screen door knob. "You look like you're sick, Mom. Let me come in."

Dee frowned, her thin eyebrows drawing almost completely together. "I wasn't stopping you."

Dare's relief washed over him like a cool shower spray. His mom might be mad at him, but she wasn't being unreasonable. If he thought about it, he could see where her worry was justified. Society didn't take well to people who lived outside its accepted norms.

But she didn't know Carter or Eddie. If she did, she'd see that they were worth any risks he took.

Dare entered the house. His mom stepped back and he noted the trembling of her hands. "Can you tell me what's wrong?" Had he done this to her? Guilt slammed into him. What if he'd given her a heart attack? Was that what was happening?

Dee leaned against the wall. "I don't know. I had my usual checkup yesterday and Dr. McCarthy prescribed me a new blood pressure medicine, and he gave me a steroid for my joint pain along with a new pain medication. I've had the steroids before. I don't know."

Dare guided her over to the couch. "I'm going to call your doctor's office. Give me just a minute."

It proved fruitless, since the office was closed. "Damned doctors hours. I want them. Must be nice to be able to work four and a half days a week."

Dee was on the couch, her eyes closed when Dare walked into the room. For one second he panicked, then he saw the rise of her chest as she took a breath. "Hey Mom, where's your new meds?" he asked quietly. If she was asleep, he didn't want to wake her.

But she opened her eyes immediately. "By the bed. What did the doctor say?"

"The office is closed."

Dee closed her eyes again. "I should have known that. I've been going there forever."

"It's all right. Just rest." Dare went and found her medicine. He sat on her bed and started Googling each one, after which he checked for drug interactions. "Bingo," he muttered. One of the drugs, he was surprised to see, was an antidepressant. It hadn't been given to his mom by her regular doctor, either.

Dare took the two medications that shouldn't have been prescribed together into the living room with him. "Mom, these aren't supposed to be taken together." He handed her the two bottles.

Her gray complexion turned to an odd shade of pink when she saw that he'd handed her the anti-depressant. "Oh. I—" Dee glanced up at him, her mouth open but no words coming out.

"Mom." Dare sat beside her and took her closest hand in his. "It's okay to take medicines like this if you need them. There's no shame in it."

"There is," she argued. "For me, there is. I've tried for so long to be strong but sometimes I want to stay in bed and cry for days."

Dare was close to his mother. How had he missed this? "Since when?"

Dee went back to studying the bottle. "Always. Your dad knew. He said it was just part of being a woman. I loved your dad, but he was very old-fashioned."

"How did I not know this, Mom? I'm a crappy son to be blind to it." Dare didn't want to make it about him, he just had to know why he'd never caught on.

"No, you don't understand. I didn't at first, either. Depression is an insidious monster that hides in your head. I think people who suffer from it the most are the same people who everyone else sees as the happiest, most out-going people." Dee shook the bottle of pills. "We compensate. We hide. We don't want anyone to now our dirty secret. Dr. McArthur doesn't even know about these. I use a different pharmacy for them, too. That's how ashamed I am of being this weak."

"You're not weak, Mom." Dare took the bottles from her. "Would you think I was if our situations were reversed?"

"It's never that simple, Dare." Dee let herself be pulled into a hug. "I wish it was as easy as saying you're right, but the truth is we're always so much harder on ourselves than we are on others. Even knowing that, I can't help but be ashamed of this. My parents would have been mortified."

"Your parents have been gone a long time. Where did you get the anti-depressants from?" he asked.

"The walk-in clinic," Dee said. "I've been going there to get them for a few years now."

And he'd not known until now. It didn't matter. He loved her more than any person in the world. "Are you going to take it wrong if I suggest seeing a real therapist? No one else would have to know. You should tell Dr. McArthur though, at least if you have meds."

"Oh, I couldn't. I've known him for so long," Dee argued. "I'd never be able to go back to him."

They had a long road ahead of them.

"Don't feel bad, Dare," Dee said. "Parents don't tell their kids everything, especially not the bad things that make us appear to be anything less than perfect." She laughed a little at that. "We're so ignorant. I am, at any rate."

"You're not," Dare told her. "You changed your way of thinking for me. You can do it again for yourself."

Dee shook her head. "I don't know. Moms love their kids more than themselves. You might not believe that after how I acted when you came out, and today—"

"Today was a shock," Dare cut in. "I can understand that. It was a shock to me, too. I can wait for you to adjust to it, as long as you understand, I'm not giving Carter and Eddie up. They already mean a lot to me, and they feel the same way. If you eventually decide to get to know them, you'll see how easy it is to love them. If you aren't able to accept our relationship, I'll still love you. I'll still talk to you and work with you. You'll always be my Mom. Nothing can change that."

"But they'll come first," she added.

Dare couldn't disagree.

Dee sighed. "I understand. You're a good son."

"Thanks, Mom. Now, about these meds. We're going to have to get you checked out somewhere."

"No we aren't," Dee said firmly. "I won't take the pain ones. They're new, obviously. I can go back to what I had before. I'll just tell Dr. McArthur these tear up my stomach."

It was probably the best he was going to get from her on the matter. Dare stopped pushing. "Okay, but I'm staying here with you for a while, until I know you'll be fine. I don't like your color."

"I won't argue with you. It scared me, feeling this way." Dee asked him, "What about your tour? And who's in charge at the brewery?"

"I asked Archie to cancel the tour, and he's handling things."

"He's a good man. You should give him more responsibility," Dee said, echoing Dare's thoughts. "He helped you with almost everything there."

"True. I'll think about it. Do you want some water? It might help. And are you sure you won't let me take you to the clinic or the ER?"

Dee tutted at that. "Those copays are ridiculous. What did you read about this kind of interaction?"

He ticked off the side effects. "That it can cause a rapid heartbeat, agitation, trouble breathing, sweating, nausea."

"But not death," Dee pointed out.

"Well—"

"I'll take some water, and if I begin to feel worse, then I'll consider going to the walk-in clinic past the brewery."

It was as much of a concession as he was likely to get from her. "Okay. Here, let me take these medicines." He took them both. "Does it help?"

Dee nodded. "It does. I wish I'd had it years ago."

Dare put the medicines away then got them both a glass of water. He'd just handed Dee hers when his phone rang. He set his glass down and pulled his phone from his pocket. It was the ringtone he had for the brewery. "Hello," Dare said when he answered.

"Hey, Dare, I called that number but didn't get an answer and no voicemail option. Who doesn't have voicemail nowadays? That's just insane," Archie ranted. "So I'll just stay and do the tour, okay? I know it anyway, since I helped you work it out."

"Thanks, Archie, I appreciate it. You can ask Mitt or whoever you want to stay there with you, too, since Mom won't be back today." He and Archie worked out the details for the tour and Dare felt confident that Archie could handle it.

"You should do that more often," Dee suggested. "Archie's been wanting to lead the tours forever."

Jesus, he really *was* oblivious. "I didn't know that. I thought they wouldn't want to stay late."

Dee's eyes glistened as she spoke. "Dare, everyone at the brewery is proud of it and of their work. It's only natural they'd want to show it off, too."

He hadn't thought of it like that before. "Huh. You know, maybe I can talk to them, and find out who is interested in doing different things. I foresee an employee meeting in our very near future." And he saw a way to spend more time with two men he was growing to care very much for.

Chapter Fifteen

Eddie wasn't the only one surprised when Dare came to the hotel.

"Mom's feeling better," Dare informed them. "And you should know we talked. She knows about us. It was rough, and she's still leery. She'll come around, though."

"Wow." Eddie gestured to the small table. "There's Chinese if you want some. We have plenty. Sit down and tell us what happened."

Dare gave him and Carter a kiss first. They all sat at the table, and Dare told them about the confrontation with his mother in between him taking bites of food. When he was finished, Eddie couldn't deny that he worried his parents wouldn't handle it so well. Still, Dare had been incredibly brave.

"And you think you aren't strong," Carter said. "Dare, you've got to be the strongest man I know in some ways."

Eddie thought so, too. "I agree. I'm scared to tell my folks, but I will soon. Mom is going to want to come out here. She's already been nagging me since she found out about Carter. I won't hide you, Dare. That's bullshit and dishonest, and you deserve better."

"You can do it in your own time. I won't be offended," Dare told him.

"My own time is coming up quick. My mom will skin me alive if I wait too long to tell her." Eddie tossed Dare a fortune cookie. "Don't forget to add 'in bed' to whatever it says."

Dare snorted and put the cookie beside his plate. "I'll do that. Y'all are heading out to Big Bend tomorrow?"

"I've got to get back to work." Eddie wished he had more time to take off. He was pushing his luck as it was.

Carter spoke up then. "He's taking me to my doctor's appointment first, then we're meeting with the cleaning crew. After that, we can—" Carter snapped his mouth shut.

"You can what?" Dare asked. "Come by to see me before you leave?"

Carter frowned at him. "How did you do that?"

Dare shrugged and pointed his chopsticks at Carter. "It was a lucky guess and yes, y'all most definitely should stop by. Mom will be fine about it. How long will you be there, Carter?"

Carter nibbled on his bottom lip for a moment, then released it. "I don't know. I want to think about things, like whether or not I should stay at my job. There are so many things I want to do and I'm limited by the five day a week ball and chain. By the time I can afford to take off and hike the Appalachian Trail, I'll need a cane and probably won't be able to go more than a yard."

"I think you're exaggerating just a bit," Eddie teased. "You know we're here for you, Carter. If you don't want to work for a while and need to figure things out, you can stay with me."

"And me," Dare offered. "I wish we could all live in one spot. Maybe someday."

"I was thinking about either trying to be a park ranger or becoming an outdoor tour guide," Carter said. "Hiking, biking, camping, kayaking, all of that and more. I could do it anywhere outside of cities, of course, and I'd have a freedom I never will if I'm not my own boss."

Eddie leaned back in his chair. "That's a good idea. I can see you doing that. You'd be a great outdoor guide."

"Thanks," Carter said, blushing lightly. He ran a hand over his shaggy hair. "Now, who is going to get rid of this for me? I can't go out in public like this."

"Why not just wear a ball cap?" Dare suggested.

Eddie and Carter gawped at him. They hadn't even thought of that.

Dare smirked. "I've got a couple of the brewery's ones out in the car. I'll run down and get them after I eat my cookie." He opened the fortune cookie. "What did y'all's say?"

Eddie had ordered a half dozen of them so they'd have extras. "Mine said you'll discover hidden talents." He winked. "In bed."

Dare seemed to be a little breathless over that. "Oh my. And yours?"

"Today is the beginning of a new adventure—in bed, but that's true of any day we're all together, isn't it?" Carter asked.

"I'd like to think so." Dare pulled the paper from his cookie. "It's—" His phone started ringing. "Oh. Hang on. It's my mom." Dare answered, and his face went ghostly white. "The brewery — What do you mean it's on fire?"

Eddie sprung up quickly, almost as if he'd been catapulted, tugging Carter to his feet as well. Anger burned in his gut. There was no way it could be a coincidence. "Call Detective Flores or Dennis. Tell them Dare's with us."

Carter started dialing.

Eddie grabbed his keys. Dare was on his feet and heading for the door.

"I'll drive us," Eddie said in a tone that made it clear he'd not tolerate any arguing. Dare was too upset to drive.

Eddie led them out of the hotel and into his truck. It was nerve-racking listening to Dare talking to his mom, and Carter murmuring to the police. Eddie wanted to know what was going on with both of those conversations. He had to be patient.

Both men got off the phone at almost the same time. "Dennis and Flores are meeting us there," Carter said. "Dare, what's happening?"

"I don't know besides the obvious. The brewery is on fire." Dare curled up in his seat. "Oh God. I hope Archie's okay. He'd have been doing the tour now. What could have happened?"

"Dare..." Carter's expression was absolutely miserable with guilt. "It could be the same guy who did this to me and who fucked up Eddie's truck."

"Why would he have done this? And how would he know we're together?" Dare asked.

Carter groaned, tipping his head back and closing his eyes. "Because if it's Mark — and I don't know who else it'd be — he knows Eddie and I have been with other men. Well, it was just Georgie for me. But Eddie's done more than one threesome."

"I have," Eddie confirmed. "This is the one that matters."

"I know I'm not a game to y'all," Dare said.

"I'm sorry you got dragged into this. I wish—"

Carter was cut off by a sharp curse word from Dare. "Bullshit. This isn't your fault. This is the fault of whoever started the fire, if it was even arson. There could have been an electrical short or a worker could have been careless somehow. We don't know what's happened."

"I'm still sorry," Carter mumbled.

"We'll get through this." Eddie turned on the street the brewery was on. Carter and Dare gasped. Orange and red flames shot out of the warehouse, through windows and the roof.

"There's no way I'll have anything left," Dare whispered. "My God. It's all burning."

Eddie stayed silent. It did seem impossible that there'd be anything left. He had to park down the street from the brewery. They clambered out, Dare shaking and his breathing loud, unsteady. Eddie took him by one elbow with the intention of guiding him and Carter past the gawkers. His heart pounded and a voice in his head was screaming at him that this was his fault—that if he hadn't been willing to bring a third man into the relationship with Carter, then Dare wouldn't be suffering this loss. He could be wrong and the fire could be a horrible coincidence. Eddie didn't think so.

"I can't believe this..." Dare shook himself. "I can't..."

Eddie and Carter exchanged a helpless look. Eddie wasn't the only one feeling guilty.

It wasn't their fault. It wasn't his, Carter's, or Dare's fault, Eddie informed that annoying internal voice. This was the fault of whoever set the fire.

"I'm sorry," Eddie murmured to Dare.

"Me too, Dare. This is…" Carter shook his head. "It's wrong."

"Neither of you did this." Dare began to jog.

Eddie had to let go of him. He and followed Dare, supporting him the only way they could at that moment.

"Dare!"

Eddie spotted Dee, hollering and waving at her son.

"Mom!" Dare called out to her.

Tears streaked her face. "Dare!"

Dare ran to her. Carter couldn't move that fast. Eddie walked with him to where Dare and Dee stood, Dare's hand on his mother's shoulder.

"Mrs. Hausemann," Eddie said, while slipping an arm around Dare's waist. The man was in dire need of comfort. Carter moved to his other side and did the same.

"Eddie, Carter," she said, nodding to them. "Thank you for bringing him. Archie's okay. He was hit on the back of the head, but Mitt saw it happen and he said he got in a good hit to the jaw of the man that did this."

"Was anyone else inside?" Dare asked.

"No. Mitt said it was just him and Archie. Mitt was going to call you right after he'd called emergency services. I just happened to show up because I… Well, I wanted to check on how the tour was going. I'm glad I did, but Dare, look at it." She waved a hand toward the brewery. "It's going to be gone."

"We can build it again," Dare told her. He stood up a little straighter. "We *will* build it again. He's not going to win."

Dee gasped and touched his arm. "You know who did this?"

Dare tipped his head toward Carter. "The same guy who did that to Carter, and who keyed a death threat into the side of Eddie's truck. It has to be."

Dee's eyes widened. "Dare, maybe—"

"Don't even suggest it," he said.

Eddie figured whatever she'd been about to say had been about Dare's relationship with them. He wished there was something he could do to help.

Dare continued speaking to his mom. "You stand by the people you care for. You don't abandon them. I know you're worried about me. What you need to understand is this guy would try to hurt anyone who Carter cared for, even as a friend. I'd like to think Carter was my friend, not just my lover."

"I am, and I'm so sorry it's caused trouble." Carter sounded miserable. Eddie knew how he felt.

"Mrs. Hausemann—"

"Dee," she corrected.

Eddie could do that. "Dee, then. I just want you to know that we care a great deal for Dare. I'm sorry this happened."

"Eddie? Is that—holy shit, Carter!"

Eddie, Carter, Dare and Dee all watched the fireman jogging over to them. Eddie's jaw dropped.

"Georgie?" Carter asked. "Georgie's a fireman?"

Georgie rolled his eyes. "I'm not always a ditzy twink. That's just to get laid. Oh, sorry ma'am," he said to Dee, putting on a bashful expression. "I tend to speak without thinking. And who is this?" He tipped his chin to Dare. "A...friend?"

Eddie stroked Dare's hip. "He's more than that, Georgie."

Georgie made very obvious eye gestures toward Dee.

"She knows," Dare informed him. "Georgie. I think I've heard of you." Dare held out a hand to shake.

Georgie batted his lashes at Dare. "Well if — "

Dee swatted at Georgie's hand. "I *know* you aren't about to make an inappropriate come on to my son."

"Your son?" Georgie squeaked. He took a step back. "No ma'am. Sorry. I've got to get back to this, but Carter, what happened to you?"

Carter was in the middle of explaining when the detectives arrived. Another fireman had joined them by then, waved over by Georgie to speak to Dare and Dee about what was happening and how their attempt to put the fire out was progressing.

Eddie was following along on that conversation. The fire was under control, the loss was substantial, and it was arson, having been set by the man who'd hit Archie with a wrench.

"Was Mitt able to give a description?" Eddie asked the fireman.

"Yes, he was."

Detective Dennis took over from there. Georgie left them and Eddie listened as Mitt was interviewed in front of them. When he described the man who'd shown up for the tour, Carter and Eddie both confirmed that it sounded like Mark.

"I guess he didn't even know I was there until I came running and shouting after he hit Archie. Before I knew it, he was tossing some of them Molotov cocktail-like things and everything started burning." Mitt rubbed his arms like he was cold despite the heat.

"I grabbed Archie and dragged him out. That's when I saw the fire burning around the outside, too."

"We believe the man who did this poured gas around the perimeter of the building before he entered," the fireman said. "He left the cans in the parking lot."

Dare was holding up better than Eddie would have in his place. Dare remained professional and calm, answering questions and asking ones Eddie wouldn't have thought to ask.

The fire was barely burning anymore by the time the detectives had finished. They arranged for Mitt to come with them to go through photos. Eddie assumed they'd have one of Mark in there somehow.

Detective Dennis pulled Dare aside and spoke to him privately. Whatever was being said, Dennis kept glancing at him and Carter.

Eddie stood with Carter and Dee, along with Detective Flores. They watched the firefighters extinguish the rest of the flames. Eddie assumed there were more than what he could see and he remarked on it.

"There are embers and such that could restart the fire, so they're soaking it all well," Flores said. "I hope Mr. Habrock had insurance."

"Of course he did. My son isn't stupid," Dee sniped. "He built this business from the ground up!"

"Yes ma'am, no disrespect intended."

Dee eyed the detective then put her on the spot. "Good. Now, you and that other detective, what are you doing to catch this man? He's obviously been getting away with everything so far. Why hasn't he been caught? It seems like it'd be wise to watch Carter since the man is stalking him."

Flores flinched under the thinly veiled accusation that she and Dennis weren't doing their jobs. "We only have so many officers—"

Dee tutted. "My Dare worked sixteen to twenty hour days for *years*."

Eddie noticed a small tic starting in Detective Flores' right eyelid. "Yes ma'am. We'll find him."

"Is it because they're gay?" Dee asked. "If Carter was a heterosexual man, would more effort be put in to this case?"

Flores' propped a hand on one hip. "Mrs. Hausemann, I assure you we are working on this case just as hard as we are any other case we have. We do *not* discriminate on the basis of anything. It's just not as simple as snapping our fingers and making the perpetrator appear. We have to know for certain who it is—which we might be much closer to thanks to Mitt—and we have to have proof he committed the crimes. Again, Mitt as an eyewitness is great. It's too bad the video cameras in the brewery were probably destroyed. Once we have a description from Mitt and hopefully a confirmation via photo, we can distribute it to the local news channels along with a request that people call us with leads. We will find him. We're doing our absolute best to do so."

"Well, forgive a mother for wanting her son safe," Dee told Flores. "I will always fight for Dare."

"As a mother should," Flores agreed.

Detective Dennis and Dare had finished their conversation and walked back over. "I'm sure Mr. Hausemann will be hearing from the arson investigator, even though this seems like an obvious case. For insurance purposes, everything will need to be laid out clearly." Dennis addressed Eddie and Carter then. "Mr. Hausemann, Mr. Canales, please be very careful and aware of your surroundings at all times. Since there's a good chance Mr. Habrock was followed to and from your hotel at some point, you might want to consider staying elsewhere. I've advised Mr. Habrock that his home may not be a safe place for him until we catch whoever did this."

"We know who did it," Carter muttered.

Dennis nodded. "Maybe, but we have to be able to prove it in a court of law. When we get the fingerprints back, that may help. Hopefully we'll have caught this guy by then."

"Hopefully?" Dee repeated.

"Mom," Dare warned. "Not now, please."

The detectives and Mitt left.

"You and Carter should leave," Dare said out of the blue. "Take him and go to Big Bend. Surely that would be safer than here. Does Mark know where you work?"

"Are you breaking up with us?" Eddie blurted out, surprised at how the idea hurt.

Dare looked at him like he was crazy. "What? No! I just meant, the cops said leave the hotel. My place isn't safe."

"There's my house," Dee offered.

Eddie so did not want to stay there.

"No thank you, ma'am," Carter said, covering for Eddie's lack of enthusiasm for the idea. "We wouldn't want to risk bringing more trouble to y'all."

"Yeah, Mom, ixnay on that whole plan." Dare ran a hand through his hair. "I'm not breaking up with y'all. I just want you both to be safe, and if Mark, or whoever this is, doesn't know where you are, that'd be great. I'll get a room at a different hotel or stay with Mom. I don't think it'll be me this nutjob is gunning for."

"Was that what Detective Dennis was doing, warning you about the potential dangers?" Eddie asked.

Dare grimaced. "Oh yeah. He seems nice enough I guess, but he wanted me to understand that hanging around y'all was a risk. I told him I didn't care. No one is going to scare me away from living my life again. Not a disease, not an ex, not some screwed up stalker, and not myself. I will *not* cave because it's the easy way out."

"I wouldn't blame you if you wanted to, but I'm glad you don't," Eddie told Dare.

"Same," Carter added.

Eddie touched Dare's shoulder. "You could come with us."

"No, I wish I could but I can't. I have to deal with the fire department, and the police, my employees—" Dare sighed. "There's a lot to be done. A lot I have to decide, too. Once that's taken care of, maybe I can learn to hike."

"Carter has a doctor appointment in the morning, and we have to meet with the cleaning crew," Eddie reminded Dare.

"That's right. I forgot. All of this has just overwhelmed me. My business…gone," Dare finished with.

"We'll help you any way we can." Carter took a step closer to Dare. "When everything is finished here, we'll go sit down somewhere, get some pancakes and coffee, and talk. What do you say? Dee, you're welcome to come, too."

"I think I should go home and let you three talk." Dee kissed Dare's cheek. "Call me if you need me. You can come stay with me if you want to."

"Thanks, Mom. Let me walk you to your car."

"We can follow behind. Safety in numbers," Carter explained.

Eddie and Carter trailed along then walked with Dare back to the parking lot.

It was going to be a long night.

Chapter Sixteen

Carter woke up when Eddie shut the truck off. He blinked the sleep out of his eyes. "I'm really fond of your RV."

Eddie smiled at that. They were both exhausted, having stayed with Dare at the brewery until everyone cleared out. It did appear that the building was going to be a total loss.

Carter rubbed his cheeks and yawned. "I can't believe it's not even dark yet. I'm so tired."

"We didn't sleep last night. Both of us are ready to crash for a while. Have you gotten any messages from the cleaning crew?"

Carter checked his phone. "Nah. Probably won't hear from them until tomorrow. I need to call the apartment manager and see what I can do about my lease there. I still had several months to go on it."

"They'll probably want you out of there, which will work in your favor." Eddie got out.

Carter did, too. He wondered when he'd finally stop hurting. He straightened the Dare's Pale Ale hat he was wearing. "Heard from Dare?"

"Not since the last time. He's got to be swamped with everything going on. I feel like shit over him losing his brewery." Eddie got their bags out of the back seat. "It's good to be home."

Carter wasn't sure where his home was anymore. He didn't think it was a place, not for him. More and more, he believed his home was wherever Eddie and Dare were.

The RV was hot so Eddie cranked the AC down to a lower temperature. "I need to go check in at headquarters, then I'll be back. If I don't do it now, I'm likely to fall asleep and get fired for not coming back on time. You want to go with me?"

Carter glanced at Eddie's bed. It was calling his name. "No, I think I'll wait here."

"Lock up behind me then get some sleep. I'll join you as soon as possible." Eddie gave him a chaste kiss and Carter watched him leave.

He locked the door and leaned his forehead against it. He listened as Eddie started the truck, then drove away.

The past week had been hell. Everything but his personal life was a complete mess. He needed to find a solitary place to sit and think about his future. Maybe, even though his ribs were sore, he could take a walk tomorrow, get outside. It felt like forever since he'd been able to hike. He wasn't capable of doing much, but he could damn sure walk.

With that decided, Carter felt a little bit better about the future. He rubbed the back of his neck, then froze, not even daring to breathe when a creaking noise behind him sent a jolt of terror through him. Though it was one of the hardest things he'd ever done, he turned around—and found himself staring at Mark.

An eerie smile curved the man's lips. Mark's hair was sticking up in patches, a scruffy beard on his face, his clothes dirty. "Hello, Carter."

Carter's fingers tingled. *Breathe.* He did, trying to appear calm.

Mark canted his head to one side. "I didn't mean to hurt you. I wasn't expecting you home yet, then…there you were. Do you know I tried? I really tried to prevent this. I even left, but California couldn't seduce me away from you. I had to come back. Once I gave in to it—once I accepted that you and I were an inevitability—things became so much easier."

Contrary to the utter panic he felt, and the almost irresistible urge to scream and run, Carter very slowly reached behind him while talking. "Easier? How did things become easier? You hurt me, and you did horrible things to my friends."

"Friends?" Mark snarled, the smile vanishing in an instant. "You forget that I know what a slut you are." Mark took a step toward him.

Carter fumbled for the lock. There were other RV campers not too far away that other rangers lived in.

Mark ran the back of his knuckles over Carter's cheek. "Easier because I understood, finally, that I don't need the medications. There's nothing wrong with me. I just need you. Now that you know how far I'll go for you—how much I value you—you'll love me. No one else will do the things for you that I'll do."

"Like burn a man's business down?" Carter snapped. "How about hit an innocent man with a—" Carter's head smacked the door when Mark backhanded him. He felt his lips split again and tasted blood.

"Don't be an ungrateful shit," Mark told him in an eerily calm voice. "I can see I'll need to teach you some manners. How are your ribs, Carter? I got few good punches in there."

Which was exactly why Carter was going to try to flee rather than fight. "They're not broken."

"How did you hit your head? I didn't do that."

Carter wiped at the blood running down his chin. "I fell."

"I've seen you move. You're graceful. Were you drunk?" Mark reached for his face and Carter flinched despite his best attempt not to. Mark smiled.

"No, I wasn't drunk." He tried to turn his head aside to avoid Mark's touch. "Don't."

"Why not?" Mark grabbed his chin and wrenched Carter's face around. He tightened his hold until pain radiated out from beneath it. "You're mine now, Carter. No one else gets to have you."

Carter found the lock, his shaking hand finally landing on it. He gave it a twist while Mark leaned in and licked his face. Carter's stomach heaved. He scrambled behind him for the doorknob, hoping Mark was distracted by lapping at his face. It dawned on him as he turned the handle that Mark was licking his blood.

Carter shoved the door open with all his might, leaning back as he did. He yelled at the top of his lungs as he tumbled out, Mark falling with him. "Help! Someone—" They hit the ground, Carter first, and pain exploded throughout his body when Mark landed on him.

"You fucking bastard," Mark snarled. He slapped Carter again.

Carter wheezed, in so much pain the slap was nothing. He wasn't giving in. He kicked and forced air into his lungs so he could yell again.

"Hey! What's going on?"

Mark scrambled off him. Carter lay on the ground, stunned and confused. Someone knelt over him and he shouted, trying to swing his right arm for a punch.

"Dude, calm down. I'm not that guy who was hitting you. Chill, okay? Just calm down."

Easier said than done. But Carter tried, and after a while — he had no idea how long — he was able to stop freaking out. "Call Eddie," he whispered to the young man bending over him.

"I'm Lem, and I don't know who you're talking about," Lem said.

"Park Ranger Eddie Canales."

Lem puckered up his lips, which made him look like he just sucked on a lime. "Oh. That guy. My girlfriend thinks he's hot. I don't like him."

Carter refrained from rolling his eyes. "I can promise you he doesn't lust after your girlfriend."

Lem was brighter than he seemed. "Oh! I didn't know — wow. Okay, so you're his boyfriend? Who was that?"

Carter closed his eyes as a wave of pain rolled through him from his chest to his knees. "Stalker. Please, get my phone — " Carter could do that himself. His ribs screamed in protest when he raised his arm.

"I'll get it." Lem plucked the phone from his pocket. "Lucky you got signal here. Eddie, right?"

"Yes," Carter whispered. "Eddie."

"Do you want to talk to him, or you want me to?" Lem asked.

"Either." Carter wanted to sink into unconsciousness.

"It went to voicemail."

Carter groaned and opened his eyes. "He's checking in at headquarters."

"Well, why don't I call them? I bet someone can patch me through. You want to get up?"

Carter didn't think he could, not without more help than Lem could offer. "No. Just, please, get Eddie on the phone."

"Sure." Lem muttered to himself, then there was silence.

Carter heard the ringing tone faintly. It stopped and Lem asked to speak to Eddie Canales.

"What do you mean he's busy? I'm at his RV and someone just attacked his—" Lem flapped a hand at him.

Carter tried to shake his head and mouth *no*. He didn't know if Eddie was out. They were always careful around his coworkers.

"His friend. There was a guy beating up his friend. Well *duh* I just said I'm at his RV! The guy was hitting this other guy who was already beat up. I yelled and he ran off." Lem sighed dramatically. "Keep up with me here, dude. Who do you think would have run off? The bad guy! Probably because I'm so intimidating."

Carter thought it was more likely because of the gun Lem had tucked into his waistband. As far as he knew, it was illegal to fire a gun in a national park, but you could bring one. Which made no sense to him at all. He supposed Lem didn't want the rangers to know he had the weapon on him.

Lem asked for Eddie again. "Fine. You go do that, but meanwhile there's a guy here hurt that needs help."

After he hung up, Lem shook his head. "I got the dumbest ranger in existence. Hey, do me a favor.

Don't narc about this, okay?" He touched the butt of the gun. "It isn't illegal for me to have it. I just don't want them watching me like a hawk because of it. There's this bobcat on the loose that attacked a little girl. I just feel safer carrying this on me."

"Firing it here's illegal," Carter said.

"Don't care. I'd rather get fined then killed by a bobcat." Lem untucked his shirt so that it draped over the weapon. "You aren't dying, right?"

Carter would have laughed had he not been in so much pain. "No. That guy, his name is Mark. He did this, hid out at my apartment and attacked me about a week ago. Mainly bruised ribs is the worst of it."

Lem snorted. "You're not too bright, letting him get you the same way twice."

Carter couldn't argue with him. It was the truth.

A few minutes later, he heard an engine. "Is that Eddie?"

Lem put a hand over his eyes to shade them. "It's someone. I can't see who. Driving an old truck."

"Eddie."

"Guess so then." Lem stood up.

Carter heard the slide of the truck tires on gravel and a siren, though he had no idea where that racket came from.

Because most importantly, he heard Eddie calling out his name, and Carter knew he was finally safe. He let the darkness take him away.

* * * *

Eddie's heart almost gave out on him when he saw Carter on the ground. He slammed on the brakes, putting the truck in park at almost the same instant. Eddie scrambled out and ran then, aware only of

Carter. He hit the ground on his knees, bending over his partner. "Carter, Carter! Honey, look at me!"

"Dude, he was just talking to me. He said it was his ribs."

Eddie glared up at the kid. "Lem, right?"

Lem nodded. "Yeah, and if you don't want everyone knowing you're..." He wiggled one hand from side to side in the air. "You might wanna tone it down. There's another ranger—oh, there's a shitload of 'em pulling up."

Eddie didn't give a damn what anyone else saw. He focused his attention back on Carter. "Honey, come on. Let me see those pretty eyes. Carter, please," he rasped.

"Canales, step back and let someone else check him. You're not thinking clearly."

As much as Eddie wanted to argue with his supervisor, he didn't. Eddie wasn't functioning past the fear he was experiencing. He started to stand up. Carter opened his eyes.

"Oh thank God, Carter." Eddie gently stroked Carter's cheek. "I'm so sorry. I shouldn't have left."

Carter's poor lips were bleeding, but he still tried to smile for Eddie. "Lem told me I was stupid."

Eddie would be speaking to Lem about that later, when there weren't any witnesses.

"Canales."

Eddie glanced up at his supervisor, Mara Thompson. "Ma'am, I'm not moving until he does."

Thompson raised both eyebrows at him, then walked to Carter's other side. She squatted beside him. "I'm going to check your pulse."

"It's just my ribs. They were already bruised."

"All of you looks like it was bruised," Thompson said. She put her fingers on Carter's pulse at the base of his neck.

Eddie held Carter's hand. He noted the handprints on Carter's cheeks. If he ever got a hold of Mark— "It was Mark, wasn't it?"

"Yeah. It was him."

"I saw the guy, too," Lem bragged. "Ran him off."

Eddie saw the tell-tale bump under Lem's shirt. He imagined he knew what had scared Mark, and he was damned glad Lem had been armed. Otherwise, who knew what Mark would have done.

"Call the detectives."

"I will," Eddie assured Carter. "Though with Mark being out here, it's going to be one of us that finds him."

"Not you," Thompson said. "You are not to be involved in it if we send out a search party for him."

Which Thompson promptly ordered done a few minutes later, after Eddie told her the whole story about Mark.

"We'll have the Texas Rangers here shortly, too— and a tracking dog. We'll find him. Meanwhile, let's get Carter here to a hospital."

Carter groaned when he was lifted into the back seat of Eddie's truck. That's when Eddie saw that he'd busted open the stitches on his head, too.

"Got to get you're noggin' restitched, honey."

"Urgh." Carter panted shallowly. "Hurts."

"I know, baby, and I'm sorry." Eddie once again wished for a smoother ride, not that he had any option. He drove Carter to the hospital in Alpine.

"We're making a habit out of visiting hospitals," Eddie joked lamely.

Carter gave him a weak smile.

Eddie parked the truck right in front of the emergency room. They could ticket him or tow it if they wanted to.

The orderly who came out to tell him to move it stopped and shook his head at Eddie. He held out his hand. "Just give me the keys then."

Eddie tossed them to him. He got Carter out, wincing when Carter whimpered and moaned piteously. "Sorry, honey. Gotta get you inside."

They made it into the ER. "Could use some help," Eddie snapped.

"Well, there was an orderly," the woman behind the counter said. She picked up the phone. "Send a wheelchair down please."

In short order, Carter was being taken off for another round of X-Rays or CT Scans, maybe both. Eddie sat down in the waiting room. He called Dare first.

"What's happening?" Dare asked immediately.

"Mark," Eddie answered. "But it's over. Carter is going to be okay. He has to be. He's getting tests run and an examination right now."

Dare gasped. "I'm on my way. I have to be there."

Eddie smiled even though he was worn thin from worry. "Be careful. I can't have you getting hurt, too."

"I will be careful. No more driving and talking— unless it's an emergency, or you need to talk?" Dare offered.

"I'll wait to do that when you're here." Eddie reminded Dare to be careful then they ended the call.

Next was Detective Dennis. "Where is Mark?"

When he answered, Eddie told him Mark was out there and maybe the detectives should talk to the Texas Rangers or something and get this shit done already.

"I get that you're tired and worried, Mr. Canales. We'll handle it from here."

Eddie hung up. The police hadn't handled it well in the first place. He was too angry to be rational. Too worried.

An hour and a half after Carter had been wheeled away, a nurse poked her head in the room. "Mr. Canales?"

"Yeah," Eddie said, standing up.

She smiled prettily at him. "Mr. Hausemann is asking for you. He's already been interviewed by the police about the assault, though actually, it was the Texas Rangers in there with him. Anyway. If you'll follow me, I'll take you to his room."

Eddie was very relieved to hear that. "Thank you."

Carter may have been a little more bruised and his lips had swollen again, but he was the best thing Eddie had ever seen. "Hey, honey."

Carter touched his lips. "This again."

Eddie winced in sympathy. Carter had a slight lisp this time, probably because the splits were worse than before. They had to be painful. "They'll be down in a few days."

The nurse straightened Carter's sheets. "I'm D'Anna and I'll be on shift until midnight. Mr. Hausemann should be released by then. His doctor's already given Mr. Hausemann his results, so I can tell you what he said, if that's okay with Mr. Hausemann? That way you wouldn't have to do the talking," D'Anna added for Carter.

"'Kay."

With Carter's permission, Deena explained that Carter had mainly just bruised his ribs again. There was no serious damage. He'd hurt for a few weeks but he'd be better.

"We're going to give you a prescription for pain meds, but don't take them unless you have to."

"He won't. Is there anything wrong with his other pain meds?" Eddie asked.

D'Anna wanted to know what they were and what milligram. Eddie couldn't remember.

"Well, call and let me know that information. If it's not as good as what the doctor was going to give, I can send the prescription to whatever pharmacy you want me to."

"Thanks." Eddie pulled a chair up so he could sit by Carter. "He's going to be released then?"

"Probably be a couple of hours. You know how that goes. Hurry up and wait." D'Anna left, after promising to do what she could to expedite the paperwork.

"Dare's on his way," Eddie told Carter. "I'm going to find us all a room somewhere tonight."

Carter didn't like that idea. "No. Let's go home."

"To the RV?" Eddie asked. "But Mark was there."

Carter narrowed his eyes. "I'm not losing my second home to that asshole."

"We'll make sure he never sets foot near it again," Eddie vowed. "It's your home, too, and Dare's, if he wants to share it." That Carter considered his RV home touched Eddie deeply. "I bet Mark's in jail before we get out of the hospital. He doesn't know that area, and unless he was carrying a couple of jugs of water, he'll be dehydrated and maybe even have a heat stroke in a matter of minutes or hours."

"Maybe he'll be bobcat food," Carter said. "Fuck. That's mean."

Eddie didn't think so. "Nah, but he'd probably make the cat sick."

Carter squinted. "Don't make me laugh. It hurts."

"I should check in and see if he's been found." Eddie shook his head. "Man, I can't believe Lem of all people showed up to scare Mark off. Lem's not fond of me because—"

"His girlfriend thinks you're cute," Carter finished.

"Yeah, that. He had a gun."

Carter nodded.

"Pretty sure he along with everyone else there knows I'm gay, so maybe Lem will get over the girlfriend thing. If not, oh well. Lem and she are only camping out for a few more days then they'll be gone." Eddie leaned over and pressed his cheek to Carter's. "I'm so pissed off at myself for not checking the RV out. I didn't think Mark knew about it. Guess he followed us at least once. But you know what? I think he's about to be caught. He's done too many stupid, criminal things, and you just don't fuck around and get the Texas Rangers after you. Might as well surrender at that point and be done with it."

Eddie sat up and Carter stared at him. "I do believe that," Eddie reiterated. "He can't last out there and he has no idea what he's up against." He winked at Carter. "So, were the Texas Rangers sexy?"

Carter grinned, which had to hurt. He winced. "Yeah. But not as sexy as my guys."

"Well then, that's all right." Eddie took out his phone. He had a text from Dare saying he was under an hour away. "He must be haulin' ass. Oh wait. No, Alpine is closer to Odessa. Dare'll be here in a bit. Nothing about Mark. Let me try calling Thompson."

The call went to voicemail. Eddie left a brief message asking for an update before hanging up. "Want to watch some boring hospital TV?"

"'Kay."

Eddie scooted his chair around a bit so he could see the TV screen better. "All right. Hurt guy gets to pick the viewing." He didn't care what they watched. Eddie was just glad to be there. He owed Lem a great big thank you for chasing Mark off. Maybe he'd give him a free season park pass, pay for it out of his own pocket. God knew Carter was priceless. Lem would probably be happy though.

Eddie settled more comfortably in the chair and groaned when Carter put the TV on one of the music competition shows. Well, he'd told Carter he got to pick, hadn't he?

Chapter Seventeen

No one with a lick of sense messed with the Texas Rangers. Even Dare knew that. As he watched Carter sleep in the hospital bed, Dare kind of hoped Mark gave the lawmen attitude. It'd serve Mark right to get his butt beaten.

That kind of thinking just leads to more anger. Let it go. It's in the hands of someone else now.

"Here's his release papers," Nurse D'Anna said. "And here's the wheelchair. Going to wake sleeping beauty up?"

"Yes, thanks." Dare took the papers and D'Anna went over them with him and Eddie.

The orderly helped Carter to get into the wheelchair once Eddie woke him up. Dare carried the bag with Carter's belongings in it. He was wearing sweats and a tank that Dare had brought for him. Well, for himself, but Dare was more than willing to share.

"It's about an hour and fifteen minutes to Big Bend," Eddie said. "You have a smoother ride, so Carter should go with you. Y'all can follow me."

"Okay." Dare pulled his car around to the front of the hospital. As he did, he saw a man being wheeled in on a gurney. Several uniformed officers were with him. *Texas Rangers. I wonder.*

Eddie and Carter were both staring hard at them. One Ranger nodded at Dare's men. Eddie held up a hand, like he was asking Rangers to wait. They slowed down, and Eddie hurried over to peer at the man being wheeled in. He recoiled pretty quickly.

Dare wasn't sure what that meant. He got out and opened the door for Carter.

"They found him," Eddie said quietly. "I'm glad. He's in bad shape. Carter nailed it. Mark ended up finding that bobcat we couldn't catch. The Rangers did that, too."

"It's...bad?" Dare asked, feeling rather stupid after he said it. Hadn't Eddie just said Mark was in bad shape?

"Yeah. Cat got to his throat." Eddie shuddered. "One of the Rangers shot the bobcat."

Those were both things Dare didn't want to see the results of. "I'm glad it's over."

"We all are. I feel... You know, I thought I'd feel ecstatic, but I didn't. It's all just such a waste. Not of an attractive man, but of a human life. And I wondered if he has a family that loves him, that'll be heartbroken over this." Eddie sagged a little, stooping his shoulders. "I'm calling Mom tomorrow and telling her. I want my family to love y'all, and that has to start with them getting to know you both, which they can't do until I'm up front with them."

"We'll be right there with you," Dare promised.

Eddie gave him a tremulous smile. "Thanks."

Dare helped Carter into the car, then jogged around and took his own seat. "I'm glad you're okay. A little more bruised but essentially okay."

"I am, and me too." Carter hissed as he leaned his seat back. "Can't wear the seatbelt. Don't hit deer or hogs."

"I won't." Dare was glad Carter dozed on the drive. He knew Carter would have been trying to talk otherwise, and those split lips looked painful.

It seemed like the drive to Big Bend itself was shorter than the drive they had once they were in the actual park. Having to poke along at slow speeds was hard on Dare's lead foot. He did tend to speed unless he used the cruise control, which he promptly set on the park property.

Eddie's RV wasn't very big. Dare didn't mind. He wanted to be close to Eddie and Carter after the scares they'd all had. Dare waited until Eddie went into the RV and came out a couple of minutes later with an "All clear," for him. Together they helped Carter inside.

"This is nice," Dare said, taking in the interior of the RV. It had light paneling on the lower half of the walls then a pretty flower-patterned wallpaper on the top part of it. The floors were a mix of wood and carpet. It was very clean and compactly designed. "Wow. I never knew these were so homey. I wonder what the bigger ones are like."

"Getting ideas?" Eddie asked in what sure sounded like a hopeful tone.

Dare knew he was blushing. He could feel it. "I—maybe? I have to figure out what to do about the brewery. If I want to rebuild or do something else. I'm leaning toward rebuilding, but keeping it smaller. I don't want work to be so all-consuming like it was.

But I just don't know yet. There are a lot of things to consider." Like his employees, his mom, and his men, and his own desires. "I think it would be a good idea if we could just spend some time together for a little while. Get to know each other better, and give us a chance to see what we want."

"I want you and Carter," Eddie stated firmly. "I don't need time to think about that."

Carter mumbled something that was, Dare thought, an agreement there.

Dare held up one hand because both guys were staring at him with hurt in their eyes. "I meant with our careers. I wasn't doubting this relationship."

"Oh." Eddie grinned. "Well then, that's a good idea."

"Glad you think so." Dare took a seat on a barstool beside the small kitchen island. "This has a fully working kitchen?"

"And bathroom," Eddie told him. "With water."

"Smart alec." But Dare laughed, delighted to be teased.

"How long can you stay?"

Dare considered Eddie's question. How long was too long? "I'm not sure. There are things I still have to take care of because of the fire, so I'll have to go back to Odessa at some point. At least for the day."

Eddie and Carter just had a way of looking at Dare that made him want to do anything he could to make them happy.

"I figured we could see how this goes. Three men in such a small place... Maybe we should spend your days off at my house—or I shouldn't stay here as often." Dare blinked at the scowls his comment seemed to have caused.

Eddie got up and marched right over to him. "Don't you think you've already made a commitment to us?"

Dare swallowed and didn't miss the way Eddie's gaze dropped to his throat. "I—it wasn't about that. I just didn't want to wear out my welcome. Too much too soon, something like that. It—mmph."

Well, that was a fabulous way to be shut up. Dare clutched at Eddie's shoulders and let the man have what he wanted. What did he have to hold back anyway? Dare was so close to loving them, would the push over into that emotion be so difficult?

Eddie pressed into the kiss, making Dare's lips tingle. He whimpered and didn't care that he did. Eddie was taking him over and it was a divine experience. Dare parted his legs, allowing for space that he hoped Eddie would fill.

He did so smoothly, sliding in, pressing the hot bulge of his cock against Dare's.

And Dare decided it didn't matter if it happened quickly or other people said it was too soon. Maybe he'd fallen in love with Eddie and Carter before they'd ever had sex. Maybe that was what Eddie meant, because Dare had given them a level of trust he'd never shared with another man.

His heart knew. It'd known all along. So had his body. It had just been his brain that had kept fighting.

Dare gasped as he tipped his head back. He was trying to get the words out. Eddie began kissing a path down his throat. When he sealed his mouth around Dare's Adam's apple, Dare had to postpone any speech. Eddie sucked, and Dare felt the pull of that hot mouth all the way down to his dick.

Eddie cupped him there, squeezing just a little, enough to make Dare want to beg.

Dare *would* beg. He had no problem with that at all.

He didn't have to. Eddie finished sucking and moved on to fucking. He had Dare turned over ass-up on the stool in seconds. "Can you see good, honey? Going to watch me fuck Dare until he comes all over my bar stool?"

Carter's lisped, "Yes" had Dare's body heating with even more intense desire. He wanted Carter to fuck him, too, and the things he thought of the three of them doing made Dare's cock so hard he wanted to shout.

Eddie reached around him and worked Dare's pants open. "This okay?"

"Yes, please," Dare whispered. "Just fuck me. I want it. I want you and Carter and everything we— Oh God," he drawled as Eddie pushed a wet finger into his ass. He must have had lube somewhere close by. Dare didn't know or care as long as Eddie kept filling him up.

Eddie pushed down on Dare's lower back and at the same time slipped a second finger into him.

Dare purred like he never knew he could and arched into the fingering, especially when Eddie caressed his prostate. Dare was so glad that little nugget was in there.

Dare turned his head so he could watch Carter. To his surprise, Carter was watching him in return—not what was going on at the south end, either. Carter locked gazes with him and Dare moaned just from the intensity between them.

"That's it, Dare. Remember who belongs to you, who you belong to."

Dare hadn't forgotten, but he'd given his men a scare by accident. He wasn't going to argue now.

And he sure wasn't going to do so when Eddie pulled those fingers free, then pressed in with that fat dick of his.

Dare panted and his vision blurred. The position he was in allowed for deeper penetration, and Eddie was already long enough to begin with. Dare felt like that heavy cock was working in all the way to his soul.

"God. Dare." Eddie pushed in the last few inches. "Better hold on."

Dare grabbed the legs of the barstool just as Eddie withdrew almost all the way.

Then it was a hard drive back and Eddie was right, it was a good thing Dare was holding on. He couldn't do anything else but that and stare blindly in Carter's direction.

Eddie didn't once slow down. He thrust into Dare over and over, filling Dare then leaving him completely a few times, too. Dare melted. Pleasure couldn't possibly describe what he was feeling. That was too tame a word for it.

And when Eddie reached under him and fisted his cock, Dare's eyes crossed and his breath stuttered.

Eddie pumped hard, both hand and shaft. Dare didn't know how he made the sounds he did. Raw, organic sounds of ecstasy bubbled from his lips.

His climax tore through him, jarring him, shaking him with a rapturous sensation that had to have shot out from his pores. Dare was dimly aware of his cock spurting, of Eddie's hoarse shout, the hot jets of cum pulsing into his ass.

It was on the tip of his tongue to confess his feelings. Dare refrained then. He wanted to tell Eddie and Carter when they wouldn't have cause to wonder if he was sex-addled.

Eddie pulled out. Dare closed his eyes for a moment but snapped them open when he felt fingers entering him again. Eddie had licked him after coming in him before, and now he was fingering him. Dare thought a certain man of his had a cum fetish.

He let Eddie help him over to the couch. To his surprise, Eddie settled him with his butt close to Carter.

"In case he wants to play. Do you, Carter?" Eddie asked.

Dare was certainly not going to have any inhibitions left before long. In fact, he looked forward to losing them one by one.

* * * *

He couldn't help it. Eddie was scared spitless when he dialed his mom's number and that fear coalesced into a hard lump in his belly when she answered.

Because he wasn't backing out. He was going to tell her. He might lose some of his other family members over this but Eddie believed his parents would come around even if it took a little while. They loved him.

And Dare's mom loved him. Yeah, she disowned him for years.

But she came around.

Would she have if he hadn't been diagnosed with cancer?

Jesus, I'm going to make myself crazy!

"Mom, I—"

"Not even a hello first?" she asked. "This must be bad."

Shit.

Carter took his free hand and Dare moved behind him on the bed. Dare began rubbing his tense shoulders and neck.

"It's not bad. I think it's great, but you and Dad might have a problem with it."

His mom hesitated before saying, "Just tell me and quit drawing it out."

Eddie closed his eyes. He saw his mom's face twisted with disappointment so he opened them right back up. "You know about Carter."

"Yes, is he okay?"

"Mark, the guy who hurt him... He was arrested." And still alive, much to everyone's surprise. "But there's more to us than that. It's me, Carter, and Dare. And we..." Wow, his chest was tight, like his lungs were too big for his rib cage. "We're all together and going to stay that way. We're committed and...and everything."

"I don't understand."

"I don't know how else you want me to explain it, Mom. We aren't a couple, we're...three."

"That isn't right, Edward, and you know it."

His heart broke a little. "Yes, it is. It's very right. Nothing has ever—"

"A man should commit to one person. One, Edward. I would not tolerate your father wanting another woman! How can you say you respect or love—?"

"Because I do," Eddie snapped. "This isn't about you or dad or the relationship y'all have. This is about me and Carter and Dare. We fit together."

"It's wrong and I will *not* approve of it."

"You don't have to. It's happening anyway. I just wanted to let you know and offer you a chance to meet the two men I love."

"You do not love both of them. Either of them if you can—"

"You love me?" Dare whispered in Eddie's other ear.

Eddie blocked out his mother's ranting and covered the speaker on the phone. "Yes, I do. Does that...? Is it too soon for me to say so?"

"Ith not," Carter said. "I love you too, Dare. And you love uth."

Dare bobbed his head. "I do. I love you both. I... Eddie, let me talk to your mom, please?"

Eddie figured there was nothing to lose at that point in regards to her. She was still angrily ranting at him. "Are you sure?"

Dare held out his hand. "Yes."

Eddie gave him the phone.

"Mrs. Canales, this is Darren Habrock and please, you can listen to what I have to say before you go off on me. Your son is an amazing man with a heart big enough to love two men. Carter and I are lucky enough to be those two guys. You did a wonderful job of raising him, but I'm going to tell you something. If you want to lose your son, keep it up. And give my mother a call. I'll send you her number."

Dare put Eddie's mom on speaker.

"You are a rude man! Talking to me like that—"

"What about how you're talking to your son," Dare retorted. "And you're trying to break up a relationship and hurt three people because you're being narrow-minded!"

"I can see there is no point talking to you. You are not a logical man."

"No, I'm a man who followed my heart, and I'm glad I did." Dare looked at Eddie and saw the love there in his eyes. "I wouldn't change it for anything, and maybe someday you'll be able to love your son unconditionally like you should, rather than judge him because he isn't doing things the way you want him to."

Eddie's mom disconnected the call.

"She loves you," Dare said. "She wants what's best for you like all good moms do. She just doesn't understand yet that her idea of best isn't the only way to go." He kissed Eddie's cheek. "It'll be okay. I'm going to send her Mom's number, and, just in case your mom thinks she can get out of calling her, I'll give her number to my mom too. We've got this, Eddie. We do."

Eddie was going to believe that. He had to. He could live without his family in his life, but he wanted it all—his men, his family, all of the joys and trials that came with both.

So he would have faith, and he'd send cards and call on his days off. If his mother hung up on him... Well, that was on her. He would do his part to make things work.

Epilogue

One month later

Carter could finally take a deep breath without so much as a twinge of pain. He was relieved, to say the least.

And he had a plan to seduce his men into putting out for him. Eddie had been gentle but firm when it came to sex. Until Carter got a doctor's release for full activity, Carter had been restricted to hand and blow jobs. Those were great. He loved them, but he was ready for more. If the hospital hadn't called to report that the doctor who'd gone over his scans in Alpine discovered torn cartilage between his ribs, Carter would have gotten his release sooner.

He had it now. Carter laid it out on the bar of the RV. He had their backpacks ready and Dare should be in from Odessa soon. Eddie would be getting off work in twenty minutes or so.

They were going hiking. Carter was taking them out for two nights into the beautiful wild country of Big Bend. And they were all damn well going to enjoy it.

Dare arrived first, barreling through the door with a big smile on his face. "Carter!" He was always so enthusiastic when he returned from a trip.

"Dare!" Carter returned, opening his arms for a big hug. "Come see what I've got," Carter sang, pointing to the paper. "A full medical release!"

Dare licked his lips. "Oh yeah?"

"Yeah." Carter then pointed to the backpacks. "I also have these ready."

Dare glanced at the packs. "Am I ready for this? Those are the overnight packs."

"You'll be with two experienced hikers, one who will be an outdoor tour guide in a few months and the other is the sexiest park ranger in the world."

"I heard that," Eddie said as he came through the doorway. The past month had been hard on him with his mother continuing to harp about his relationship. At least she was talking to him, and she was in for a surprise because Dare's mom had had enough of Eddie being hurt. She was going to talk some sense into her.

"Eddie, Carter got his medical release." Dare did a wiggly dance and leered at Carter.

Eddie laughed and strolled over. He grabbed a handful of butt on each of them. "And I see the overnight bags are packed. I'm assuming there's lots of lube in them."

"Along with everything else we need," Carter assured him. "So you two sexy guys get ready. I even laid out clothes for y'all, and put your hiking boots by the bed."

"Eager, aren't you?" Dare asked.

Carter grinned. "Why wouldn't I be? I get my men and hiking, my three greatest passions. Now hurry up! I want to go."

Eddie gave his butt a squeeze then Carter stood at the bar watching Dare and Eddie poke and push each other on the way to the bedroom. Sometimes they were just like two overgrown kids. Carter was, too. Being serious too often had to be unhealthy.

"Need me to come pull y'all's shoes off?" he called out. The two yeses didn't surprise him at all. Carter walked to the bedroom then helped his men get undressed before assisting them in getting their hiking clothes on. "You two are fine as fuck."

"We are," Eddie preened. "So are you, honey."

Dare pinched Carter on the butt, shocking him. Dare snickered. "The look on your face!"

Carter rubbed the spot on his backside that still tingled. "You just wait. Tonight I'm going to have you."

Dare's eyes rounded and Carter leaned over to lick his neck. The salty taste of him was addictive.

"None of that or we won't be leaving here," Eddie groused. "Let's get our bags."

Carter stepped back and made sure Dare got a good look at the way his dick was tenting his shorts. "After you."

They picked up their backpacks then headed out after locking the door. Maybe it wasn't strictly necessary. Mark was in a coma and unlikely to ever be a danger to them or anyone again. Another park ranger was living in an RV beside them. That was one of the reasons Carter wanted to have his men out on this hike. They had to be careful about how much noise they made when they were fucking, because RV's weren't soundproofed as well as they'd have liked.

Carter was going to get them far enough away that they wouldn't have to worry about being loud. "Let's move it." He set up a steady, brisk pace. "If y'all want to be a part of my dirty plans…"

Eddie and Dare kept up. They laughed and talked and enjoyed being outside, being with Carter and each other. It was the most perfect day in his life, Carter decided when he stopped them as the sun was beginning to set. "This is good."

"Are we supposed to be in this area?" Dare asked.

Carter peered at Eddie. "You want to answer that?"

"We can, because I'm here. Now we'd better get the tent up before it gets dark. It's easier to do it now than with the lantern."

It took them less than two minutes to have the tent up. Dare went about setting out the food and drinks for dinner. It wasn't anything extravagant, but hearty and healthy food to replace the calories they'd burned.

Carter set out what they would need in the tent. Lube, wet wipes, the two plugs he'd bought that he was going to surprise Eddie and Dare with. Hiking while wearing them wasn't going to happen, but he and Dare could sleep with them on. Eddie would love that.

Eddie opened the tent flap, startling Carter. He had both plugs in his hands.

Eddie's face turned ruddy. He looked over his shoulder. "Dare! Bring the food in here!"

Carter gulped. He'd seen lots of expressions on Eddie's face, but never such an intensely hungry one as he wore now—and it wasn't food Eddie was wanting.

"Give them to me," he said, coming into the tent.

Carter handed them over. "The blue is for Dare. It'll be gorgeous against his skin."

Eddie examined it. "Yeah, and the black will be great against yours. Turn the lantern up."

Carter turned it up. Dare entered the tent holding a sealed container with their dinner in it, and three bottles of water on top of it. "What—oh," he said. "I can not get naked fast enough."

He tried. Carter got stripped down almost as fast, but Dare did beat him to it.

Eddie had taken the food and drinks from Dare and set them on the sleeping bag farthest from them. "Carter, how much do you want?"

"All of it." He'd longed for the rough handling he hadn't been in any shape for after being hurt. "Spank me. Fuck me. Let me fuck you," he said to Dare.

"Kiss him," Eddie ordered. "Show him how much you want him."

Carter had Dare in his arms just as soon as he could. He wanted everything with Dare, with Eddie. They had him, heart, body and soul.

When Dare was breathless and trembling with need, his dick hard and wet-tipped, Carter kissed his way down Dare's chest, over the taut ridges of his belly and to his pretty shaft. Eddie guided his head and Dare's penis. Carter opened his mouth, sucking, licking, so happy to be where he was, with his men.

He took Dare's length into his throat and swallowed around it. Dare pulled at his hair.

"I'll come. Oh my God, Carter, I'll come!"

"You'd better not," Eddie told Dare.

But he pushed Carter's head down further until he could suckle Dare's sac. At the same time, Eddie poured lube down Carter's ass crack. Carter moaned, knowing what was coming next. Eddie pushed a thick finger into him.

"Yes," Eddie hissed. "Oh honey. This is going to feel so good."

Yes, it is!

"Dare, kneel down and present your ass for Carter. He hasn't gotten to fuck since he and I met. Give him everything you've got."

Carter wasn't sure who that last part was meant for, because Eddie tossed the lube and it landed by Carter's hand.

Dare got down and put his pretty butt up in the air, spreading his knees wide and exposing his hole for Carter. Carter fondled Dare's ball for a minute while Eddie kept fingering him. When Eddie curled his finger and rubbed over Carter's gland, it gave him the impetus to bring such pleasure to Dare.

Carter squeezed out some lube and rubbed it over Dare's pucker. He pushed two fingers in slowly, listening to the wanton sounds Dare made.

Eddie worked another digit into Carter, and it was so good Carter had to pinch himself, literally, to push back his climax. When Eddie touched his gland again, Carter knew he was going to have to speed things up.

Dare took a third finger with little resistance.

Eddie withdrew his digits from Carter's hole. "Fuck him, Carter. Mount him and pound his ass while I spank yours."

"Sounds perfect," Carter scraped out. He stopped stretching Dare, withdrawing his fingers and lining up his cock. "Better brace yourself, Dare. This is about to get rough."

"Thank God," Dare said. He wiggled his butt.

"Do it, Carter." Eddie urged, caressing Carter's hip. "Fuck him as hard as you can."

Dare's moan was loud and long.

"I think he likes that idea," Carter concluded. He sure as hell thought it was a brilliant plan. "Grab your dick when you're ready to come." And without further delay, Carter thrust, sinking into the heated embrace of Dare's body. "Fuck," he drawled. He wasn't going to last long with that velvety grip surrounding his length.

"That's it," Eddie crooned. "Ride him hard."

Carter withdrew almost fully. That was when Eddie swatted his backside, bringing a sting to his skin. "Eddie, again," Carter pleaded. He wanted to fuck Dare. He wanted to be spanked. He wanted to be fucked —

Eddie grabbed Carter by the nape and held onto him while slapping his ass every time Carter slid back. It was the perfect blend of pleasure and pain. When Carter's ass was on fire from the swats and his balls were drawing up to push out his release, Eddie knelt behind him. Carter's next move backward impaled him on Eddie's thick cock.

Carter shouted, bucking between his men. Dare keened and reached for his own shaft. Eddie slammed into Carter, who in turn drove his dick into Dare harder and faster.

Eddie pushed at Carter's back.

Carter folded over Dare.

Eddie covered them both and fucked Carter like a machine.

The pleasure being pumped into him from his dick and ass overwhelmed Carter. He came in a blinding flash of white, a roaring in his ears that only later would he realize was a mixture of Eddie and Dare's voices.

And as he lay between them, plugged and sated, Carter was filled with excitement over the future they would share.

It would be challenging, and worth it. They were going to make it work. He started making plans to take his men with him along the Appalachian Trail.

About the Author

A native Texan, Bailey spends her days spinning stories around in her head, which has contributed to more than one incident of tripping over her own feet. Evenings are reserved for pounding away at the keyboard, as are early morning hours. Sleep? Doesn't happen much. Writing is too much fun, and there are too many characters bouncing about, tapping on Bailey's brain demanding to be let out.

Caffeine and chocolate are permanent fixtures in Bailey's office and are never far from hand at any given time. Removing either of those necessities from Bailey's presence can result in what is known as A Very, Very Scary Bailey and is not advised under any circumstances.

Bailey Bradford loves to hear from readers. You can find her contact information, website details and author profile page at http://www.totallybound.com.

Totally Bound Publishing

Home of Erotic Romance